"I take it you [...] *wanted to say* [...]

Chance said.

Jenny lifted her gaze and met his evenly. "I just wanted to make sure we were clear about something."

"What's that?"

"You and I..." Jenny waved her hand dismissively, as if no other words were necessary.

"Yes?" Chance prodded.

"There is no you and I, no us, no anything, correct? We already established that." Jenny tried hard to sound matter-of-fact.

He returned her look with a perfectly bland expression. "If you say so, darlin'."

"I do," Jenny said firmly.

Chance grinned. "Last time I heard those two words said with so much passion, I was standing in a church."

Dear Reader,

With Mother's Day right around the corner, Special Edition commemorates the warm bonds of family. This month, parenthood brings some unlikely couples together in the most wondrous ways!

This May, Sherryl Woods continues her popular AND BABY MAKES THREE: THE NEXT GENERATION series. THAT SPECIAL WOMAN! Jenny Adams becomes an *Unexpected Mommy* when revenge-seeking single father Chance Adams storms into town and sweeps Jenny off her feet with his seductive charm!

Myrna Temte delivers book three of the MONTANA MAVERICKS: RETURN TO WHITEHORN series. In *A Father's Vow,* a hard-headed Native American hero must confront his true feelings for the vivacious schoolteacher who is about to give birth to his child. And look for reader favorite Lindsay McKenna's next installment in her mesmerizing COWBOYS OF THE SOUTHWEST series when a vulnerable heroine simply seeks solace on the home front, but finds her soul mate in a sexy *Stallion Tamer!*

Listen for wedding bells in *Practically Married* by Christine Rimmer. This final book in the CONVENIENTLY YOURS series is an irresistibly romantic tale about an arranged marriage between a cynical rancher and a soft-spoken single mom. Next, Andrea Edwards launches her DOUBLE WEDDING duet with *The Paternity Question.* This series features twin brothers who switch places and find love— and lots of trouble!

Finally, Diana Whitney caps off the month with *Baby in His Cradle.* In the concluding story of the STORK EXPRESS series, a *very* pregnant heroine desperately seeks shelter from the storm and winds up on the doorstep of a brooding recluse's mountain retreat.

I hope you treasure this book, and each and every story to come!

Sincerely,

Tara Gavin
Senior Editor & Editorial Coordinator

Please address questions and book requests to:
Silhouette Reader Service
U.S.: 3010 Walden Ave., P.O. Box 1325, Buffalo, NY 14269
Canadian: P.O. Box 609, Fort Erie, Ont. L2A 5X3

SHERRYL WOODS
UNEXPECTED MOMMY

SPECIAL EDITION

Published by Silhouette Books

America's Publisher of Contemporary Romance

SILHOUETTE BOOKS

ISBN 0-373-24171-2

UNEXPECTED MOMMY

Printed in U.S.A.

Books by Sherryl Woods

SHERRYL WOODS

Whether she's living in California, Florida or Virginia, Sherryl Woods always makes her home by the sea. A walk on the beach, the sound of the waves, the smell of the salt air all provide inspiration for this writer of more than sixty romance and mystery novels. Sherryl hopes you're enjoying these latest entries in the AND BABY MAKES THREE series for Silhouette Special Edition. Her next single-title romance, *Amazing Gracie,* will be released in mid-May 1998.

Dear Reader,

From the moment fourteen-year-old Jenny Runningbear burst onto the scene in *The Rancher and His Unexpected Daughter,* I knew she was going to be a powerful force to be reckoned with. Feisty, stubborn and willful even then, she was destined to have a book—and a love—of her own.

With her loyalty to her Native American heritage, with a dedicated attorney for a mother and Harlan Adams for a stepfather, how could Jenny grow up to be anything other than an incredible, special woman?

As a teen, she'd stolen Harlan's pickup and turned his life upside down, before he managed to tame her and marry her mother.

Now in *Unexpected Mommy* it's payback time for all that mischief she stirred up way back when. Jenny is a dedicated teacher, whose first day of school is turned into chaos by none other than an Adams.

Petey Adams is the grandson of Harlan's bad-sheep brother, who'd been sent away from the family ranch in disgrace. Petey and his daddy, sexy Chance Adams, are dead set on revenge, and Jenny is caught squarely in the middle.

But no one is better suited to matching wits with a couple of troublemakers than Jenny, and no one is destined to fall harder than this reformed bad girl who's learned all about loyalty and love the hard way.

I hope you enjoy this very special woman and this latest continuation of the AND BABY MAKES THREE series.

Sheryl Woods

Prologue

"It was the prettiest slice of land the good Lord put on this earth," seventy-five-year-old Hank Adams whispered, his voice frail, his eyes glazed over with a faraway look. "Did I ever tell you about White Pines, son?"

Chance held back his impatience and forced a smile. "Only about a million times, Daddy." Seeing his father's disappointment, he quickly added, "But I never tire of hearing about it, you know that."

"Is the heat on?" his father asked, shifting subjects as he often did these days. He shivered and pulled the two layers of blankets a little tighter under his chin. "You sure that danged furnace is working?"

The furnace was pumping out enough heat to sizzle meat as far as Chance was concerned. The blazing fire only added to the oppressive, stifling atmosphere in his father's small Montana cabin. But ever since Hank Adams's health had begun to fade a few months earlier, it seemed he couldn't stay warm enough. The only thing that seemed to distract him for long was reminiscing about the home he'd left behind decades earlier back in West Texas. The bitterness seemed to Chance to be as fresh now as it must have been on the day his daddy had been chased off by his older brother, Chance's uncle, Harlan Adams.

"The furnace is turned up to near eighty," Chance said. "You'll be warm in a minute, Pop. Tell Petey and me another story about when you were growing up."

"Yeah, Granddad," Petey said enthusiastically. "Start at the beginning. Tell us about how my great-great-granddaddy came all the way from the South after the Civil War and built this big old mansion just like the one he'd left behind."

"You could probably tell that one yourself," Chance said, grinning at his son and ruffling the boy's shaggy sun-streaked hair that so closely resembled his own.

Most of the time lately Petey's moods ranged from difficult to impossible. He'd never been able to sit still for much more than a minute, but recently, ever since his grandfather had come home from the hospital to die, Petey rarely left the old man's side. It was as if he knew there was only a little bit of time left to absorb all the tall tales and family history.

What worried Chance was that he was also latching on to all his grandfather's bitterness and resentment. The fight for a share of White Pines wasn't Petey's. If there was going to be a battle—and that was a mighty big if—it was Chance's to wage.

He glanced at his father and saw that he was settling back, searching his memory for stories to keep Petey entertained or, more likely, to incense him.

"Now let's see," his father began. "That would have been in the spring of eighteen hundred and sixty-nine."

Petey's eyes widened as if he were hearing the date for the first time. "Wow! That's like a hundred years ago, huh?"

"More than that, boy. The war was over and the family's home had been wiped out by them damn Yankees. They plundered it first and then burned the whole place to the ground. That was that hellion Sherman who was responsible," he said, adding a colorful curse or two to emphasize his poor opinion of the man.

Then he went on. "Your great-great-granddaddy was little more than a boy then, not even eighteen, as I recall. He'd been through more at that age than most men live through in a lifetime. He knew things would never be the same for any of them there, so he packed up his mama and his two sisters and headed west to start over."

Hank's voice seemed to fade. It was hard to tell if he'd forgotten the rest or was merely tiring.

"Where was his daddy?" Petey coached.

"Killed in the war."

"Did they have any money?" Petey asked, prompting his grandfather to tell his favorite part of the story.

"Some that his mama hid away, along with some jewelry. They sold that so they'd have a little nest egg for startin' over. They sold it all but a ruby-and-diamond pin."

"The one you brought with you to Montana," Petey proclaimed triumphantly. "Can I see it?"

"It's locked away safe, boy. It's your daddy's to give to his wife, if he ever marries again," he said with a pointed glance at Chance. Then his eyes turned misty again. "Lordy, that pin is something, though. I can remember my mama wearing it when she got all dressed up sometimes. Looked like a little basket of ruby red rosebuds and sparkly diamond baby's breath. There was many a day when your grandma Lottie wanted me to sell it so we'd have a little something in the bank, but I wouldn't do it. That pin was the only legacy I had from my ancestors. Now it's your daddy's and someday it'll be yours."

Chance let his mind wander as the familiar tale washed over him. He knew the story practically word for word. He'd been hearing it since he'd been younger than Petey. Just as his son was now, he'd been enthralled by the adventure of the move from the South all the way to West Texas, by the building of White Pines and the founding of the town of Los Piños. He had a feeling his father had embellished the story a bit over time, inventing a few tussles with Indians and thieves that hadn't actually occurred. Even so, it was a heck of a story.

He could envision the grand house that had been built as an exact replica of the mansion that had been destroyed. He could see the spread of land abloom with bluebonnets and crossed by sparkling streams and shaded by pines and cottonwoods.

"Why'd you ever leave, Granddaddy?" Petey asked. "How come you came to Montana?"

Hank Adams sighed heavily at the question and his eyes darkened with anger. His agitation was as great now as it probably had been decades earlier when he'd been forced from the home he loved. Chance didn't like seeing him get himself so stirred up over something that was long over with.

"Leave it be for now, Petey," Chance said. "Your granddaddy's tired."

"Not tired," the old man said, his chest heaving as he tried to draw in a ragged breath. "Still makes me madder than a wet hen when I think of it, that's all."

"Then don't think of it," Chance advised, regarding him worriedly. "Just rest."

"Can't rest until this is settled," his father retorted. "Should have done it years ago."

"Done what?" Petey asked, clearly sensing a new twist was coming, one they hadn't heard before.

Chance knew it, too. He'd expected something like this his whole life, dreaded it.

"I should have gone home," his father said. "I should have claimed what was mine, instead of letting that low-down scoundrel of a brother of mine take it all."

"You'll go," Chance soothed, knowing it was a lie. If Hank hadn't mustered the gumption for the fight years ago when he'd had his strength, he'd never do it now. As he had with so many things, Hank would want someone else to handle it for him.

"Harrumph," his father responded. "Not me. It's too late for me." He reached out and seized Chance's hand. "You, though, it's not too late for you to go. You and Petey. With your mama and your wife both gone and me breathing my last any day now, there'll be nothing to hold you here."

The mention of his late wife silenced Chance as nothing else could have. The wound of Mary's death was still too raw and painful, even though it had been more than a year now since the flu had turned into pneumonia and a three-day blizzard had prevented them from getting the medical help she desperately needed. It had been his fault. He should have ridden out at the first sign she was sick, instead of listening to her reassurances she'd be fit as a fiddle again in no time.

Losing his sweet, gentle Mary had cost him his soul and hardened his heart. Had it not been for Petey, he might very well have lost his mind. Petey's out-of-control behavior was fair warning that he had to go on living in the here and now. Hank's illness had been the clincher.

What his father said was true enough, though. Chance had come to hate Montana and its bitter winters. He liked ranching, but there were other places he could settle down and start over. If Hank hadn't been too ill and too ornery to move, Chance would have packed them all up and headed off to start over months ago. Once his father died, there really would be nothing left to keep him here. Still, as shiftless and irritating as Hank could be, Chance didn't want to think about not having his father bossing him around and telling his tales.

"You're going to live to be a hundred, you old coot," he said, squeezing his father's callused hand. "You're too stubborn not to."

A terrible racking cough seized his father just then as if to give lie to Chance's prediction. When it was over, his father's brow glistened with sweat. His color was ashen.

"Listen to me," he said, his voice raspy. "You go to Texas. You have as much right to White Pines as anyone who's left there. Maybe Harlan's still alive, maybe he's not, but that house, that land, was my heritage as much as his. He stole it from me. Take it back, Chance. Take it back for me. It's the only way I'll ever rest in peace, knowing that you and Petey have what's due you." His eyes glittered feverishly. "Promise me, son. Promise me."

Chance feared the cost of an argument would be too great. "I promise you, Daddy. Petey and I will go to Los Piños," he said, though he wasn't sure he ever intended to follow through. He wasn't certain he had the strength left to carry on an old family feud.

His father's grip tightened. "Don't say that just to pacify me, son. A promise made on a man's deathbed has to be kept. It's the next thing to making a promise to God. You understand that, don't you?"

Hank had been well into his forties when his only son was born. He'd already been set in his no-account ways. Over the years Chance had fought with his father as often as he'd agreed with him. Their rows had been loud and legendary in these parts, but he loved the old coot.

"I understand," he said softly, reaching for a damp cool cloth to wipe his father's brow.

"Petey?" the old man whispered.

Petey crept closer. "I'm here, Granddaddy."

"You're a good boy, Petey. Wild and spirited, just the way I was, but you have a good heart, same as me. Don't let anybody ever tell you otherwise."

Chance put a hand on his son's shoulder and squeezed. Tears were spilling down Petey's cheeks. It was clear he sensed the end was near.

"Granddaddy, don't die," he pleaded. "Please don't die like Mama did."

Hank Adams gave Chance's hand one last squeeze, then reached out his arms for his grandson. Petey climbed onto the bed and hugged him back fiercely, refusing to let go.

"Shh, boy. Don't cry for me. You have to be brave for your daddy. Make sure he takes you to Texas, okay? I won't be here to see that he does, so you'll have to do it for me."

"Daddy!" Chance warned.

His father shot him a final stubborn look. "Just making sure you keep your promise, son. Now you won't be able to look Petey in the eye if you don't."

Stunned and infuriated by such a sneaky tactic, Chance glared at him. "You're a manipulative old son of a gun. You know that, don't you?"

His father cackled. "Hell, boy, I'm an Adams. That's our heritage as much as White Pines and cattle."

He sighed then and closed his eyes. Chance had to coax a tearful Petey away from the bed.

It was a few more hours before Hank Adams died, but those were his last words, and they echoed in Chance's head in the days to come.

By the time school was out for the year, he'd made up his mind. He put both houses—his and his daddy's—on the market, packed up his and Petey's belongings in the back of his pickup, paid one last visit to the cemetery where Mary and his mother and father had been laid to rest, said goodbye to neighbors he'd known all his life and headed south.

"It's going to be just like it was for my great-great-granddaddy," Petey said, bouncing in his seat with excitement. "We're having a real adventure."

"Yes," Chance agreed with one last look at his

past in the rearview mirror. Either they were going to have an incredible adventure, or they were heading straight for disaster. He wasn't quite prepared to lay odds on which was the more likely.

Chapter One

Sweet heaven, it was true. Jenny Runningbear Adams stood just inside the doorway to her fourth-grade classroom and tried very hard not to panic. All around her chaos reigned, which just proved there was always a payback for the sins of the past. Years of childhood misdeeds were returning to haunt her.

If her stepfather could see this, he'd laugh till his sides split. Harlan Adams just loved irony. He'd always told her that one day she'd run across a child as impossible as *she* had been. Apparently this school year she was about to be confronted by a whole classroom of them.

She stared around her in horror and wondered what had possessed her to shift from teaching history and current events to eighth graders. She'd had some idealistic notion that elementary-school students would be more receptive, easier to mold. Obviously she'd lost her mind. The evidence of that was right in front of her.

The opening-day bell had barely rung and already chairs had been upended. Papers were strewn from one end of the dingy room to the other. Graffiti had been scrawled across the blackboard in every shade of chalk. Unfortunately, not even half the words had been spelled correctly. Stacks of textbooks she had neatened herself only yesterday were tumbled in disarray. Pandemonium was in full swing.

A freckle-faced girl was huddled at her desk sobbing as she clutched one fat braid in her hand, while the other bobbed on the left side of her head where it belonged. She looked like a lopsided doll after an encounter with a four-year-old's scissors.

A pack of boys was circling the girl's chair, whooping as if they'd just succeeded in scalping her. It was an image that sent a particularly nasty chill through Jenny's part-Native American blood.

She took in the entire scene, drew a calming breath and prayed for patience, fortitude and maybe just a little divine intervention. At this moment she deeply regretted ever thinking of teaching as a way of giving something back to the community and sticking a little closer to home than she'd been in recent years.

More than one person had warned her that this would not be as simple as dealing with a bunch of hardheaded, shortsighted congressmen or even the eighth graders she'd had the year before. She had scoffed at that. Lobbying on Capitol Hill had been a three-ring circus. Eighth graders had been discovering the power of hormones. Fourth graders were little kids.

Well, that particular horse was out of the barn. She was here, under contract for another school year, nine endlessly long months. The prospect of day after day of *this* made her shudder. The only way around it was to seize control now, right this second.

"That's *enough!*" she said just loudly enough to be heard over the uproar. That particular tone, lethally calm, had quelled many a rioting group in the past, although most of them had been adults caught up in a frenzy of advocacy of some Native American cause or another. She waited with some trepidation to see if it worked with this pint-size mob.

If it didn't, she could always inform the principal that she'd had a sudden mental breakdown and it would no longer be safe for her to be left alone with young children. Patrick Jackson disliked her so much he'd accept the explanation without batting an eye. Besides, teaching was her second career, anyway. She could always find a third. Change was good. In fact, at this precise moment, it struck her as both positive and inevitable.

As she contemplated her future with some enthusiasm, two dozen pairs of eyes turned in her direction, surveying her, sizing her up. The sobbing child with the unfortunate haircut watched her hopefully.

"Everyone find a chair, get it behind a desk and sit," Jenny instructed. When no one moved, she added, "Now!"

Slowly but surely she detected signs of movement. First one chair was scraped into place, then another and another. She caught a couple of guilty looks being exchanged as she crossed the room toward the chubby-cheeked victim of the morning's torment.

She hunkered down in front of her and grasped her trembling hands. "Sweetie, it's going to be okay," she soothed, though she was certain of no such thing.

"No, it's not," the girl said, her voice thick with choked-back tears. "My hair is g-g-g-gone."

"But now you can have a whole new hairdo," Jenny said cheerfully. She smoothed a tendril of hair away from the child's flushed cheek. "Look at my hair. It's short. Takes me two minutes to wash and dry it. No tangles, either. And you have a lovely face. Short hair will show off your beautiful eyes."

The girl blinked owlishly at that. "You think so?" she asked hesitantly.

"I really think so."

"But what is my mom going to say?" she asked miserably. "My hair's been growing practically forever. She'll kill me."

"I'll speak with your mother," Jenny promised.

"After all, this wasn't your fault. It's not as if you lopped off that braid yourself. What's your name?"

"Mary," the child said. "Mary Rose Franklin."

"Well, Mary, why don't we go and make a call to your mother right this minute and see what we can do about this." She smiled at her. "Just think how envious all your friends are going to be that you got to miss the first day of school."

Mary sniffed and managed a faltering smile of triumph for her now subdued classmates.

Jenny took the child's hand and led her toward the door, then paused as she recognized the danger in her plan. The class was very likely to erupt into chaos again the instant her back was turned.

She turned slowly back to face the other students. She doubted she would ever learn which student was responsible for this disaster, but maybe she could transform the incident into a lesson for all of them. If she didn't take control of these nine-year-olds today, it would be a very long year.

Or a very short one, if she followed through on seeking new employment. *Any* new employment. Once the principal saw Mary's new haircut, he might very well encourage Jenny's career change. In the meantime, though, she leveled a stern look at her young charges.

"When I get back here, I expect to find you exactly where I left you," she said. "And I expect to find the person responsible for chopping off Mary's hair writing an apology to Mary."

Several boys snickered. Jenny scowled.

"On second thought, perhaps all of you should be writing that apology," she said firmly. "Even if you didn't cut her hair, you all stood by and watched it happen. That makes you accessories. I'll explain exactly what that is when I get back. Then you can read your letters aloud. They had better ring with sincerity or every one of you will spend the next month in detention. Maybe longer." She scowled. "Maybe the whole semester. Have I made myself clear?"

"Yes, ma'am," a redheaded girl muttered dutifully. Her hands were folded neatly atop her desk and her expression was as solemn and innocent as a saint's.

"Yes, ma'am," several others mimicked.

Jenny sighed and decided to let the taunt pass. "You may start now." She waited until heads were bent and pencils were scratching over paper before taking Mary to the principal's office and explaining the morning's catastrophe.

Patrick Jackson peered at Jenny over the ugly black frames of his thick glasses, then glanced at Mary and sighed heavily. "I just knew something like this was going to happen the minute I heard the board had approved your transfer to this school. I would have fought it, but it would have been a waste of time. Even though you've been trouble ever since you hit town twenty years ago, your family has too much influence for me to win."

She ignored the reference to her family and to her

inauspicious beginnings as a resident of Los Piños. Some memories were destined to die hard.

"This is hardly my fault," she protested, instead. "I wasn't even in the classroom yet."

"My point precisely. The bell had rung. Where were you?"

Jenny stared at him incredulously. "In here with you listening to yet another explanation of my duties, along with a few off-the-cuff remarks about my lack of suitability as a teacher," she shot back.

That gave him a moment's pause. He settled for regarding her sourly. "And who's with your class now?"

"No one," she admitted.

"Obviously you learned nothing from what happened this morning." He shook his head. "It's just as I expected. You are not cut out for this."

Jenny barely resisted the urge to utter a curse that would have blistered the man's ears. After all, Mary had been traumatized enough for one morning. She didn't need to see her brand-new teacher lose her temper and punch Mr. Patrick Johnson in his bulbous nose.

She stood a little straighter and said with quiet dignity, "If you will call Mary's mother and explain what happened, I will get back to my other students."

"Go, go," he said, waving her off. "I'll speak to you again at the end of the day."

She beamed at him. "I'll be looking forward to it." He'd have to catch her first, she thought as she gave Mary's hand a last reassuring squeeze and bolted from the office.

As she raced down the hall, she listened for the sounds of renewed chaos erupting in her classroom. Instead, it was absolutely silent as she approached. She found the quiet worrisome, but she was grateful nonetheless.

Inside, Jenny scoured the room for signs of mischief. It appeared, though, that she'd gotten her message across. No one had budged so much as an inch in her absence.

"Is everyone finished writing that apology?" she asked, perching on the edge of her desk and surveying the students.

"Yes, ma'am," the same little redhead replied eagerly.

"Yes, ma'am," the others taunted in a singsong chorus.

"Enough!" Jenny said. "Who'd like to go first?"

Naturally it was that accommodating little redhead who replied.

"Fine," Jenny said. "Your name is?"

"Felicity Jackson."

Jenny winced. "Any relation to our principal?"

"He's my father," the child said proudly.

Of course, he would be, Jenny thought with a sigh. "Okay, then. Thank you, Felicity. You may go first."

Felicity's essay was less of an apology than a well-crafted crime report. Bless her little suck-up heart, she readily mentioned not only the precise details of the insult that had been perpetrated on her classmate, but the name of the boy responsible: Petey Adams.

Before Jenny could say a word, a boy—almost certainly the boy in question—flew out of his seat and aimed straight for Felicity, clearly prepared to knock the breath clean out of her. Jenny stepped in his way with seconds to spare. With one arm looped around his waist, she plucked him off his feet.

"Petey, I presume."

"You can *presume* anything you danged well want to," he said with a defiant tilt to his chin and fire flashing in his startlingly blue eyes.

Something about that chin and those eyes looked disturbingly familiar. Jenny had the uncomfortable feeling she ought to recognize Petey, especially since his last name was Adams, the same as her own.

"Petey, you and I will discuss this incident when the rest of the class goes to recess," she informed him. "In the meantime you have two choices. You can remain in your seat and behave, or you can spend the morning in the principal's office. It's up to you, but I should warn you that Mr. Jackson is very eager to get his hands on the person responsible for Mary's haircut." She smiled at the boy. "What's it going to be?"

The defiance slipped just a notch. "Might's well stay here," he muttered eventually.

"Good choice," she said, and released him to return to his seat. "Perhaps you'd like to read your apology to the class."

"Didn't write one," he said, glaring at her. "You can keep me here till I'm an old man and I still won't write one."

The belligerence took her aback. "You did hear me give the assignment, didn't you?"

"I ain't deaf."

"Then you are deliberately choosing to defy me?"

He squared his little shoulders and stared straight back at her. "Yep."

She had to admire his spunk if not his insubordination. She had a whole new respect for the teachers forced to deal with *her* through the years. How she handled Petey Adams was absolutely critical to gaining the respect of his classmates, with the possible exception of Felicity, who obviously craved the approval of all authority figures more than she wanted the friendship of those her own age. She was definitely her father's child.

"Okay, Petey, we will discuss this matter during recess."

He shrugged indifferently.

Jenny turned to the other students and called on them one by one to read their apologies. Fortunately there were no further incidents. Still, by the time recess came an hour later, she was so tense her shoulders ached. She made arrangements for the third-grade teacher to supervise her students on the playground, then returned to meet with Petey.

He regarded her with hostility. Jenny sighed. She took a moment to look over his file, which she'd retrieved from the office on her way back from the playground. He was new to Los Piños. His mother had died less than two years before, his grandfather just months ago. He was all alone with his dad, who'd taken a job as foreman of a ranch near White Pines.

Jenny recalled all too vividly her own sense of being lost and alone after her parents' divorce, when her mother had brought her from New York to this strange new place. She kept a tight rein on her sympathy, though, as she looked up and faced the boy seated in front of her.

"You're new this year, aren't you?"

"So?"

Apparently there was to be no such thing as a simple yes or no with this kid. "I remember when I went to a new school," she said. "In this very town, in fact. I wanted to make sure everybody knew they couldn't mess with me."

There was a brief spark of interest in his eyes. Jenny considered that a good sign.

"I got myself into as much trouble as I possibly could," she said, deciding not to tell him the precise nature of that trouble. Explaining that she had stolen Harlan Adams's car and smashed it into a tree when she was barely fourteen might just give this kid the idea that he'd been wasting his time chopping off pigtails.

"What'd you do?" Petey asked.

"Oh, lots of things," she said dismissively. "What I really wanted most of all was to get my mom's attention. She'd been so busy getting us settled and getting set up with her new office that she hadn't had much time for me."

Petey's eyes brightened. She had clearly caught his interest.

"Did it work?" he asked eagerly.

Jenny smiled at the memory. "Oh, it worked, all right. She was furious with me. She made me go to work."

Petey stared at Jenny, disbelief written all over his face. "But you were just a kid."

"True."

"How old?"

"Fourteen."

"I'm only nine. My dad would never make me work."

"That's what I thought about my mom. She was a lawyer, after all. I told her she was violating child labor laws, but she didn't care. She said I had to learn a lesson. She put me to work for the man whose property I damaged."

Petey considered that, then regarded her with a worried frown. "Do you think I'm going to have to pay for Mary's haircut?"

"I wouldn't be surprised," Jenny said. "It might even be good if you volunteered to do that. It would show that you're sorry for hurting her and that you know what you did was wrong."

"But I don't have any money."

"Then I suppose you'll have to do like I did. You'll have to earn it by doing chores."

His gaze narrowed. "You mean like doing Mary's homework and stuff?"

She bit back a grin. "No. I think you and Mary should each do your own homework. But maybe you could help out around her house or maybe your dad will give you extra chores at home and you can give the money to Mary's mom."

For the first time Petey squirmed uncomfortably. "You're really going to tell my dad?"

Jenny was fairly sure he'd known that was going to be the outcome from the beginning of this little escapade. Now that it was a certainty, though, he was obviously worried about the consequences.

"Actually I was hoping you would tell him yourself," she said.

"He'll be really really mad, though."

"You should have thought of that before you took those scissors to Mary's hair."

He sighed heavily, then his expression brightened. "I know. Maybe I could do chores for you and you could give the money to Mary's mom. We wouldn't have to tell my dad at all."

"Nice try, but I don't think so. After school you and I are going to go see your dad," she said firmly. "I understand he's working for a rancher right outside of town. It's on my way home. I'll drive you."

"I'm supposed to take the bus," he argued.

"We'll make an exception today."

"I shouldn't ride with a stranger. My dad said so. My granddad, too."

"I'm not a stranger. I'm your teacher."

"I don't think that matters. My dad doesn't know you." His expression brightened. "Maybe you should just write a note and I'll take it home," he suggested hopefully.

And flush it down the toilet, Jenny thought. "Nope. I want to speak to your dad face-to-face."

"Okay," Petey said, his expression sullen again. "But don't blame me if he says it's all your fault."

"My fault?"

"Sure. If you were a better teacher, it would never have happened."

Out of the mouths of babes, she thought wearily. With Petey regarding her triumphantly, she swore that if she survived this day, she was going to think very seriously about choosing another profession. Less than half a day on the job this year and she was already regretting not going into law with her mother or maybe ranching like her adoptive father, Harlan Adams. Heck, maybe even calf roping would have been a better choice. Then again, she'd tried that once at her father's insistence. She hadn't been very good at that, either.

For the rest of the day she pondered what sort of man would have a son as insightful and inventive and troublesome as Petey Adams. Just thinking about facing such a man was almost enough to make her choose to stick around school and square off with Patrick Jackson, instead. Almost, but not quite.

Ducking out would irritate the pompous principal, which was pretty good motivation in and of itself.

In fact, by the time the final bell rang, she was actually looking forward to meeting Chance Adams. She was just itching to go toe-to-toe with an adult, instead of a classroom of pint-size hellions.

Chapter Two

In retrospect, the decision to settle in Los Piños had been easier than Chance had anticipated. Even when he'd driven into town two months earlier, he hadn't been sure he would stay. He'd just meant to keep his promise to his daddy, check out White Pines and then move on if West Texas didn't suit him. In fact, if it hadn't been for Petey, he might have kept on roaming for the rest of his life. He was too restless, too soul-deep exhausted to start over.

As it was, though, he knew his son deserved stability. Petey needed schooling and a real home to come to, his own bed to sleep in. The motel rooms they'd stayed in on the road when they'd first left Montana were fine for a night or two. But they were not the kind of places where he could raise a kid.

No matter how sick at heart he was himself, he owed his son a better life than that.

He'd still been wrestling with his conscience when they'd crossed the border into Texas. He'd deliberately taken his time getting to Los Piños. They'd gone to the southeast part of the state first, taken a swim in the Gulf of Mexico, which Petey had declared way more awesome than the creeks back home. Then they'd spent a few days exploring the wonders of Houston, the biggest city Petey had ever seen, before moving on to Dallas, where Petey had wanted to see the stadium where his beloved Cowboys played. Whatever happened, Chance had wanted Petey to have his grand adventure. He'd hoped that would make up for all the grief in his young life. Two devastating losses in as many years were enough to shake up a boy's whole world. A man's, too, for that matter.

At any rate, it had been early July by the time they'd driven into Los Piños. Chance had expected to feel some sort of tug, some kind of connection to the place, but as far as he could see it was no different from any other ranching community in the West. The businesses catered to the cattlemen, nothing fancy, just good solid merchandise at decent prices.

They were just in time for the town's annual Independence Day celebration. Flag-waving families had gathered all along the sidewalks for a parade that was twice the size of the one back home in

Montana, even though the town was no more populated, at least as far as Chance could tell.

After the parade there'd been a picnic. Most folks had brought their own baskets of fried chicken, along with blankets to spread on the grass, but there were plenty of food concessions for those who wanted to buy hot dogs and fries and cotton candy.

The celebration was wrapped up that night with fireworks. Chance had choked back bile at the oft-repeated announcements that the lavish display had been donated by none other than Harlan Adams and his sons.

"Y'all be sure and thank 'em when you see 'em," the mayor said.

Petey's eyes had widened at the mention of Harlan Adams. "That's Granddaddy's—"

Fearing he'd be overheard, Chance had put a hand over Petey's mouth, cutting off the blurted remark in midsentence. It was too soon for anyone to know he was connected in any way to the powerful Harlan Adams. He wanted to size things up before he made his presence and his intentions known—if he ever did.

But hearing all that boasting had solidified one thing: he was staying. He wanted to see just how the other half of the family had thrived after running his father off. Resentment he hadn't known he felt simmered all night long.

During the day he had asked around about employment and learned that a rancher named Wilkie Rollins was looking for an experienced foreman.

"It's a small place compared to White Pines," one man told him. "Then, again, most are. White Pines is about the biggest cattle operation in the state, bar none. Harlan's got himself quite a spread out there. That boy of his, Cody, has doubled the size of it these past few years. He's a smart one, all right, every bit as sharp as his daddy."

"Is that right?" Chance said, absorbing the information about his cousin and tucking it away for later consideration. "How do I go about finding this Rollins place?"

"You can't miss it if you head west going out of town. If you come up on them fancy gates at White Pines, you've gone too far."

The directions had been easy enough to follow. The next morning he'd driven out there, talked with Wilkie Rollins and had a job and a new home by the end of the interview. He and Petey had been settled in by sundown. Petey had been ecstatic that they were staying on.

In the weeks since, Chance had been happy enough with the familiar work. Wilkie's spread was smaller than his own had been in Montana, but the man was getting too old to handle it himself. He left most of the decisions to Chance and drove into town every day to hang out with his cronies. Chance had been able to keep up with the work with time to spare to contemplate his next move with Harlan Adams.

Petey was hell-bent on charging over there and introducing themselves and staking their claim. He'd been all but deaf to Chance's admonitions that slower was better. Fortunately, despite being the next-door neighbor, White Pines was too far down the road from Wilkie's for Petey to sneak off there on his own to snoop around.

"Patience, son, patience," Chance said over and over, but he figured he was pretty much wasting his breath. Petey was intent on fulfilling his grand-daddy's last request.

Through the years Chance hadn't gotten caught up in his father's bitterness. It had always seemed a waste of energy to him. But now, the more he heard about those paragons of virtue out at White Pines, the more the high praise grated.

He wondered what folks would have to say if they knew that Harlan Adams had stolen half of that ranch right out from under his younger brother. He wondered how they'd react if they knew that Hank Adams had been sent away all but destitute. In the past two months Chance had started working up a pretty good head of steam over it himself.

While he debated the best way to go about making his presence known, he gave Wilkie his money's worth and let the idea of revenge simmer. Some of his plots were subtle and downright sneaky. Some were blatant and outrageous. All of them ended with him and Petey ensconced in that fancy house a few miles up the road from the little foreman's cottage they currently called home.

He was just trying a new scheme on for size when he glanced up from the wood he'd been chopping and caught sight of a slender dark-haired woman striding in his direction, a purposeful gleam in her eyes. Since she also had his son in tow, he suspected Petey had been up to some sort of mischief again. He'd hoped the start of school today would settle the boy down, but it looked like just the opposite had happened.

The boy was darn near out of control. He managed to find a way to do mischief where Chance would have sworn none was possible. Chance would have tanned the boy's hide, if he'd thought it would help, but his own father's lashings had never done anything except make Chance more defiant than ever. Since Petey had his temper in spades, it seemed likely he'd react the same way.

Chance wiped his brow with the bandanna he'd stuck in his pocket and stood back to watch their approach. Might as well appreciate the sight of a pretty woman while he had the opportunity. In a few minutes they were going to be on opposite sides of something or other. That much was clear from the scowl on that pretty face of hers.

She was tall, five-eight at least, he gauged from a distance, and thin as a poker in her fancy doeskin-colored linen slacks and bright orange blouse. Her black hair was cropped short as a boy's, emphasizing wide cheekbones and eyes as dark as coal. There was a hint of Native American ancestry in her angular features.

He put her age at anywhere from late twenties to early thirties. She had the brisk no-nonsense stride of a man, but as she neared, he saw that she had the surprisingly ample curves of a woman beneath that clinging silk blouse of hers. His body reacted as if he'd just spotted a primed and waiting sex goddess in his bed.

The reaction, of course, was the result of too many months of celibacy. This woman wasn't at all his type. She was way too skinny, and that determined jut of her chin warned him she'd be a handful of trouble.

"Mr. Adams," she called out as she neared. She sounded way too grim to be dropping by for the sheer pleasure of it.

"That would be me," he confirmed, glancing at Petey. When his son determinedly refused to meet his gaze, Chance looked the woman over from head to toe, hoping to rattle her. The action was as instinctive as breathing. He'd always enjoyed flirting with a pretty woman, no matter the circumstances. If he could distract her from her mission, so much the better. Instead, though, her gaze remained fixed squarely on his face as she patiently withstood the examination.

"Satisfied?" she asked eventually.

There was no hint of color in her cheeks, but Chance felt his own flaming. "Not by a long shot," he said, trying to reclaim the edge he'd lost.

She shrugged. "Let me know when you are. I can wait."

He concluded that trying to best her was a losing

te sincerity. "No, thanks, darlin'. I'm not the
it interested in dropping by for barbecue and
w."

time her gaze narrowed at his rudeness.
' she said. "And why is that?"

said it in that cool haughty way that might
ckled him under other circumstances. Chance
another smile. "That would make it seem too
like I was a guest in my own home."

cuse me?"

regarded her with feigned surprise. "Why,
, haven't you figured it out yet? I thought for
u were quicker than that."

ured out what?"

ept his gaze steady and his voice even. "That
oved to Los Piños for the sole purpose of
that big old ranch away from your daddy."

y felt a lot like kicking dust straight into
 Adams's arrogant face. Unfortunately, since
come to his house just to tell him his son
d more discipline, she couldn't see that
ng a temper tantrum herself would accomplish
It might give Petey the notion that the only
separating them were age, height and power.
dn't be a good lesson at all.

ever, forcing herself to remain calm in the
 Chance Adams's outrageous claim required
it of self-control she possessed.

whole thing was ridiculous. Of course, he
t confused. It was a case of mistaken identity

cause. "Who are you?" he asked since no one had
seen fit to fill him in.

"I'm Petey's teacher."

He'd guessed as much—Petey was coming home
from school, after all. And the woman with him had
a prim and prissy attitude about her, just like every
teacher Chance had ever had, though she was definitely a whole lot sexier than most.

"You have a name?" he asked.

"Jenny Adams."

Chance flinched. This was a turn of events he
hadn't anticipated. He'd heard all about Harlan Adams's sons. He hadn't heard a word about any
daughters. Then again, Adams was a common
enough name. Maybe she wasn't kin at all.

"Adams?" he repeated cautiously. "Any relation
to Harlan Adams?"

Her expression brightened. Those great big eyes
of hers sparkled like coal well on its way to turning
into diamonds.

"He's my father," she said with pride. "My
adoptive father, actually. I was Jenny Runningbear
before he married my mother and adopted me. Do
you know him?"

"Oh, I know him, all right," Chance said coldly.
"Or maybe I should say I know all about him, since
we haven't exactly been introduced."

"Dad!" Petey protested, tugging urgently on his
jeans.

Chance ignored him. Before he could stop himself, he blurted what he'd intended to keep secret

for a while longer yet. "Harlan Adams is my uncle. He and my father were brothers."

She gaped at that, clearly stunned. Petey looked equally shocked that his father had done precisely what he'd been warning Petey not to do.

"That's not possible," Ms. Jenny Adams declared.

"Why? Because dear old Dad hasn't mentioned his long-lost brother?" Chance said, surprised at the bitterness in his voice. Apparently Hank's resentments had taken hold, after all. "They haven't been on speaking terms in years, not since he rode my daddy out of town and stole his heritage out from under him."

Genuine bemusement washed across her face. "That's not possible," she repeated, her tone a mixture of shock and outrage. "Obviously you don't know my father at all if you think he's capable of doing something like that."

Chance forced a smile. "Oh, I assure you it's more than possible, cousin Jenny. It's a genuine fact." He regarded her with a touch of defiance. "Unless you're calling me a liar."

He glanced at his son, who was following the exchange with a mixture of shock and relief. Apparently Petey figured this revelation was the next best thing to salvation, since it had served to distract his teacher from whatever she'd been intent on saying about his behavior in school today.

Chance thought Petey's optimism was a bit premature. He doubted that Ms. Adams could be dis-

or something. Harlan had no brother she'd ever heard about. He'd taken a dying ranch left to him by his shiftless daddy and made it pay. If White Pines was legendary in Texas and Harlan was powerful, then he owed it all to the sweat of his own brow. He hadn't stolen anything from anyone. She'd have staked her life on that. She'd never met a more honorable man than the one who'd adopted her when he'd married her mother.

She supposed she ought to tell Chance Adams just how far off base he was, but the angle of that stubborn chin suggested she'd be wasting her breath. She studied that chin for just a moment and concluded there was a distinct resemblance between it and every other male in the entire Adams clan. The discovery shook her a little, because it lent just the tiniest bit of credence to his preposterous claim.

Rather than start an argument over who owned what, she said sweetly, "Perhaps I should leave you to work out those details with my father when you finally meet. I'm actually here to discuss Petey."

The man sighed and some of the arrogance drained right out of him.

"What's he done?" Chance asked as if expecting the worst. He glanced at his son. "Petey?"

Since Petey remained stoically silent, Jenny described that morning's escapade.

"I'll pay for the girl's haircut," Chance said readily enough.

"Perhaps Petey should pay for it," Jenny suggested. She gestured toward the firewood. "Maybe chopping wood, for instance, would work off some of those aggressive tendencies. Physical exertion can be very healthy." She ought to know. Harlan Adams had worked her butt off after she'd stolen and wrecked his pickup.

Chance scowled at her suggestion, clearly resenting it and her.

"I'll deal with Petey the way I see fit," he responded stiffly. "Maybe you should concentrate on getting control of your class. If you can't cope with a bunch of nine-year-olds, maybe it's time to look for other work."

Petey shot her a triumphant look. He'd predicted his father would say that very thing. Jenny refused to concede to either of them that she'd said very much the same thing to herself just a few hours earlier.

She wondered what Chance would think if he discovered that one of the ideas she'd considered was working at White Pines, the very ranch he intended to seize as his own. Maybe she'd tell her father this very afternoon that she wanted to learn everything there was to know about ranching. Then she could flaunt her own claim to White Pines in this man's face. She hadn't had a decent mental and verbal skirmish since she gave up leadership of a Native American rights organization to move back to Los Piños. Something told her that Chance Adams would prove to be a fascinating challenge.

She sighed. Her father, of course, would see straight through her. From the day he'd made her one of his heirs he'd known that what she really wanted to do with her share of White Pines acreage was put a Bloomingdale's on it. Not that she'd ever make good on the threat, but it had been a running joke between them for too many years now for him to believe she'd suddenly developed a taste for ranching.

Her future wasn't the immediate problem, though. Petey's was. She regarded Chance Adams evenly. "It's entirely up to you what you do about your son's behavior," she said. "But I will tell you now that I will not tolerate a repeat of this in my classroom. The next incident will result in a suspension. Have I made myself clear?"

His blue eyes, the exact same shade possessed by every single one of her stepbrothers, sparkled with amusement. That hint of laughter was enough to make her want to spit. Yes, indeed, Chance Adams would be a challenge and then some.

Fortunately for her, Luke, Jordan and Cody had the same kind of arrogance, the identical streak of stubbornness. She'd learned long ago to give as good as she got with the three of them. She'd even learned to do it with words, instead of fists, since not one of them would ever have dared to brawl with their much younger stepsister as they did among themselves.

Chance was once again eyeing her speculatively. "Darlin', you are the cutest little thing when you're mad," he said in a tone clearly calculated to infuriate her. "You sound all prim and fussy. I had an old-maid schoolteacher once who sounded just like that.''

Acid churned in her stomach as she fought yet another urge to retaliate with the kind of response that would have been instantaneous only a few years earlier. She was an adult now. A teacher. She was supposed to be setting an example, for goodness' sake, not rolling around in the dirt pummeling a man who'd just insulted her.

Unfortunately Chance Adams was the sort of man who would test the self-control of a saint. She hoped there wouldn't be many more encounters like this one to provoke her, at least not in front of an impressionable boy.

Maybe her desire to belt the man was plain on her face. Or maybe he knew just what the limits of her patience were likely to be, because suddenly out of the blue he sent Petey into the house. The boy scurried off so fast he left dust whirling in his wake.

It was exactly the circumstance Jenny had been hoping for. She could take an unobserved shot right at the man's chin, she thought wistfully, then gave a little sigh of resignation. She wasn't going to do it, of course.

Still regarding her with amusement, Chance Adams rocked back on his heels and looked her over again. Her skin burned every single place his glance skimmed over.

Well, two could play at that game, she thought with defiance of her own. And he was showing a whole lot more skin.

She fixed her gaze squarely on his bare chest and ogled. She let her gaze drift slowly up to that sexy stubbled jaw, then down to the golden hair arrowing below the waistband of his jeans, then up again to broad shoulders. Looking him over, no matter what her purpose, turned out to be more fascinating than she'd anticipated. Her pulse fluttered, then ran wild. He was quite a specimen.

The technique worked, though. She had a suspicion that not all the perspiration on Chance's gleaming muscular chest was the result of the hot sun and chopping wood. The muscles in his throat worked as if he might just be having the teensiest bit of trouble swallowing. If she'd had some water with her, she would have offered him a cool drink for his parched throat.

Or doused him with it.

When she'd concluded her survey to her satisfaction and his discomfort, she forced herself to look smack-dab into his eyes. "As you can see, I give as good as I get. Shall we declare a truce, Mr. Adams?"

If she'd thought her little challenge was going to end it, she could tell at once from the amusement again sparkling in his eyes that she'd made a terrible mistake. He shook his head very slowly, his gaze locked with hers.

"Not on your life, darlin'," he said slowly. "I'd say the fireworks are just getting started."

Chapter Three

Chance kept a tight rein on his desire to laugh as he watched Ms. Jenny Adams sashay off, her back ramrod straight, her chin tilted at a defiant angle. Darn, but that confrontation had felt good. He hadn't had so much fun in a long time. He couldn't recall the last time a woman had stared at him so boldly and made his blood run quite so hot in the process.

Too bad she was an Adams. Okay, an adopted Adams, technically speaking, but that still made her the enemy. He figured she was tied to his Uncle Harlan by loyalty if not by blood. Sometimes those ties were even stronger than the genetic ones a person didn't have any say over.

The squeaking of the screen-door hinges snapped his attention back to the matter that had brought the woman here in the first place. He pivoted just in time to see Petey trying to slip off in the direction of the barn to escape Chance's likely wrath.

"Oh, no, you don't, young man. Get back here," Chance commanded.

Petey took his sweet time about complying with the command. When he finally stood in front of Chance, he scuffed the toe of his sneaker in the dirt and refused to look up. He didn't look guilty, though, merely defiant. Chance figured that was an attitude that needed correcting in a hurry.

"Son?"

"Yeah?"

"That's 'Yes, sir.'"

Petey sighed heavily. "Yes, sir."

"That's better. Now look at me."

Another heavy sigh greeted that order. Chance would have smiled, but he figured it would take the edge off the stern displeasure he was trying to convey. "Now," he repeated emphatically.

His son finally darted a glance up at him. The defiance had begun to slip ever so slightly. His eyes shimmered with unshed tears. Chance fought the urge to gather the boy in his arms. It was moments like this that were the hardest tests for a father. He was torn between the discipline he knew needed delivering and the comfort and promise of unshakable love that were also required.

"I'd like an explanation," Chance told him, pleased with his calm neutral tone when minutes ago he'd wanted to shake the kid for doing something so crazy. Jenny Adams had painted an all-too-vivid picture of that distraught child with a severed braid in her hand, tears spilling down her cheeks. He winced every time he thought about it. He'd been so sure he'd taught Petey girls were to be protected, not taunted or hit. Maybe he'd been remiss in not mentioning that their hair was off-limits, too.

"An explanation 'bout what?" Petey replied.

The innocent act tripped Chance's temper all over again. "About what the dickens possessed you to cut off that girl's braid," he snapped, then sucked in a sharp breath. In a calmer voice, he added, "You had to know it was wrong."

"I suppose."

"Suppose nothing. It was wrong. It was downright cruel, in fact. It's the exact kind of mean-spirited act I've told you to protect girls from, isn't it? Even little girls fuss about their looks. Did you think for one second about how she would feel with her hair all lopsided?" He shook his head. "Obviously not. Now tell me why you did it. You must have had a reason."

Petey still looked as if he was about to cry. Once again Chance had to force himself not to kneel down in the dirt and take the boy in his arms. Mary Rose Franklin was the one deserving of sympathy here, not the perpetrator of the crime. An image of Jenny Adams's disapproving expression stiffened his resolve. He didn't intend to give her or anyone else the ammunition to accuse him of being a lousy dad.

Keeping his expression stern, he repeated, "Son, I'd like an explanation now."

"Timmy McPherson dared me," Petey said miserably. "He said if I ever wanted to have any friends at all in Los Piños, I'd do it."

I should have guessed as much, Chance told himself. It was all too typical for kids that age to set each other up to take a fall as some sort of test. "I assume you weren't counting on Mary being one of those friends," he said wryly.

Tears leaked out of Petey's eyes and spilled down his cheeks. "I didn't mean to make her cry. Honest, Dad. I just wanted to be friends with Timmy and the other guys. I'm the new kid. I didn't want them to think I was a total geek or something." His chin jutted out. "It's not like her hair won't grow back."

Chance cringed at the logic. "You don't make real friends by doing things you know perfectly well are wrong," he said. "Have you apologized to Mary yet?"

Petey looked even guiltier. "Not really. Ms. Adams assigned us to write an apology in class, but I didn't do it. I told her I wouldn't."

Chance sighed. "Why not?"

"Because it wasn't my fault, not really. It was Timmy's idea," he explained. "And then that Felicity girl ratted on me, just so she could get Ms. Adams to like her."

"Tattling's not the issue here," Chance pointed out. "And Timmy wasn't the one who chopped off Mary's hair, was he? You always have choices, son.

You could have found a more sensible way to make new friends. I think maybe you'd better go inside and write that apology now. As soon as I get cleaned up, we're going to take it to Mary and hope and pray that she and her parents will forgive you. And if you ever hope to see a penny of your allowance again, you'd better pray that whoever fixed your classmate's hair did it cheaply.''

Petey stared at him in dismay. ''You're going to make me go to her house? I have to talk to her parents, too? And give them my allowance?''

''Yes.''

''But, Dad—''

''We're going,'' Chance said with finality. ''Have that note ready by the time I'm dressed or I'll start adding days to the week I already intend to ground you.''

''Dad!'' Petey wailed.

''Save your breath, son. I've let you get away with too much since your mama and granddaddy died. It's going to stop and this is as good a time as any to be sure it does.''

''This is all Ms. Adams's fault,'' Petey grumbled, then added vehemently, ''I hate her. If you loved Granddaddy, you'd hate her, too. She's one of *them*. She deserves to have bad things happen in her class. Maybe they'll even fire her for being a crummy teacher.''

This time Chance did kneel down. He put his hands on Petey's shoulders and forced him to meet his gaze. ''I don't want to hear that kind of talk again, okay? One thing has nothing to do with the other," he said, ignoring the fact that only moments earlier he, too, had been thinking of her as the enemy. He didn't want to consider what kind of nightmarish behavior Jenny Adams would have to face in her classroom if he encouraged Petey to make her part of his grandfather's vendetta. No fourth grader in Los Piños would get an education this year.

"But she lives at White Pines," Petey protested.

"For the moment," Chance said grimly, solidifying his resolve to settle things with Harlan Adams the very instant he could come up with a workable plan. Dragging it out would take its toll on all of them.

He looked Petey in the eye. "I repeat, one thing has nothing to do with the other. She is your teacher and you will respect her in the classroom and that is final. Understood?"

"No," Petey said, his chin jutting again. "Her father is a thief. That makes her no good, too. Why should I have to listen to anything she says?"

Obviously Hank had been very thorough in imparting his resentments to Petey. Chance couldn't see any long-term benefit in allowing Petey to grow up with so much hate. If there was a score to be settled, he would be the one to do it.

"Okay, let me put it another way," he said quietly. "I am telling you that you will show respect to her in that classroom. I am your father, and if you don't obey me, there will be hell to pay. Is that clear?"

Petey blinked several times at his father's fierce tone, then bobbed his head once.

"Excuse me. I didn't hear you."

"Yes, sir," Petey mumbled.

"That's better. Now get inside and write that note. We'll be leaving here in twenty minutes."

Petey's expression was sullen, but he did as he was told. Inside, Chance watched him for a moment, his head bent over a piece of paper from his notebook as he began slowly writing the ordered apology. Chance suspected it would be lacking in sincerity, but the point was getting Petey to go through the motions. He had to understand there were consequences for bad behavior.

Chance had learned about consequences at an early age. His father had been tough as nails, impossible to please and erratic about the rules Chance was expected to follow. It had kept Chance in a constant state of turmoil. He wouldn't do the same to Petey. He intended to make sure Petey understood exactly what the boundaries of acceptable behavior were.

When Jenny Adams had been telling him how to discipline his son earlier, he'd been every bit as resentful as Petey was now. But the truth was, her words had been a wake-up call. Petey needed more parenting than Chance had been giving him. Ever since their arrival in Los Piños, he'd been too caught up in this obsession with getting even with Harlan Adams. That was no excuse for neglecting his son or letting him get so carried away with his own brand of retribution. Now that Petey knew his teacher was Harlan Adams's daughter, there was no telling what the boy would try to make her the target of his anger.

Chance resolved then and there that Jenny Adams would never have another reason to question his ability to teach his kid the difference between right and wrong. If they met again—and they surely would—it was going to be because of his plan to ruin Harlan Adams. If a few sparks happened to ignite between them in the process—and they were dead-on certain to—so much the better.

Somehow, though, he intended to keep Petey out of the middle of things. Given how well Hank had primed the boy, though, that was likely easier said than done.

The fireworks between Jenny and Chance were nothing compared to the explosion that night at the dinner table when Jenny repeated Chance's declaration about White Pines. Harlan might have been in his eighties, but he hadn't slowed down and he wasn't inclined to take any threat to the sanctity of his home lightly.

"That darn fool," he said viciously, slamming his fist on the table so hard the dishes bounced. His skin turned an unhealthy shade of red and a sheen of perspiration broke out on his brow. "Obviously Hank spent his whole sorry life filling that boy's head with lies. Now he's dead and the rest of us are left to clean up the mess he's created."

Jenny exchanged a worried look with her mother, Janet, who appeared ready to leap from her chair and go to her husband's side to calm him down. Jenny's younger half sister, Lizzy, stared at him, clearly stunned by their father's outburst.

"Maybe I shouldn't have said anything," Jenny said, regretting her impulsive relating of the entire incident. She should have known it would upset to her father. Being accused of cheating his brother out of an inheritance was not something Harlan Adams would take lightly. "I'm sorry."

He reached out and patted her hand. "Of course you should have told me. No point in keeping quiet about it. Obviously this Chance Adams intends to create a ruckus sooner or later. Leastways now I can be prepared for it. There are plenty of folks in town who were around at the time. They're familiar with the details."

"Then you really did have a brother?" Jenny asked, though that much at least seemed obvious from her father's agitated reaction.

"I did," he said tersely.

"How come you never mentioned him?" Lizzy asked.

"Jenny, Lizzy, leave it be for now," her mother warned. "Can't you see how distraught your father is already without you two stirring the pot? Give him time to absorb all this."

He waved off her concern. "I'm not half as upset as I'd be if this Chance Adams had taken me by surprise," he declared, pushing away from the table.

Despite his claim, though, he was visibly shaken. Once on his feet, he took a moment to steady himself. This time Jenny was about to rush to assist him, but a sharp look from her mother kept her in her seat.

Finally he squared his shoulders and said, "I'm going to my office. I've got some thinking to do."

"Harlan, you haven't even finished your dinner," her mother protested.

"I'm not hungry."

Her mother gave a resigned sigh. "I'll bring a snack to your office in a bit, then," she said, watching him go, her expression filled with concern.

When he was gone, Jenny turned to her mother. "I'm sorry, Mom."

"No, Jenny. Harlan's right. It's better to be prepared, I suppose." She didn't sound convinced.

"Did you know anything about this brother?" Jenny asked.

"Nothing. He's never said a word. It's as if the man never existed. I doubt we would ever have heard of him if this Chance Adams hadn't turned up."

"There's not a single snapshot in the house with him in it, I'm sure of that," Jenny said. "Remember how I used to make Daddy sit down with all the family albums and tell me who everyone was?"

Her mother smiled. "Once he made you an Adams, you went about it with a vengeance. I've never known anyone so anxious to know every little detail about their adoptive ancestors."

"I don't know why that surprised you," Jenny countered. "I was the same way about yours. It's just that you'd been telling me all those stories for years and years. Besides, I wanted to figure out which one of those sneaky Adamses stole Native American land."

She'd made the comment in jest, but her mother looked thoughtful.

"Harlan made you his heir so you'd get your share of that land back," she reminded Jenny. "Do you suppose he'll do the same thing to make things right with Chance Adams?"

"Nephew or not, Daddy didn't sound much like he thought this man had a legitimate claim," Jenny said.

Lizzy agreed with her. "In fact, I'm betting that by tomorrow he'll have the wagons circled. You'd better tell Maritza to count on every family member within shouting distance to be here for dinner. Daddy's probably calling Luke and Cody and Jordan now."

"You're probably right," her mother conceded. "In that case, I'd better take that snack in to him and make sure he eats it. He's going to need all his strength for whatever lies ahead."

By dinnertime the next day, Harlan had, in fact, gathered the whole darn clan. Luke and Jessie had driven over from their ranch. Cody, who ran White Pines on a day-in day-out basis, was there with Melissa. Even Jordan had flown in from Houston, where he'd been checking on the branch office of his oil operation for the past week. Kelly met him on the porch and they came in together.

The next generation was represented by Jordan's son, Justin, his daughter, Dani and her new husband, and Cody's son, Harlan Patrick. Cody's daughter, Sharon Lynn, was expected as soon as she closed Dolan's for the night, along with her fiancé, Kyle Mason.

Looking at the noisy gathering crowded around the dinner table, Jenny smiled. She was pretty sure Luke's daughter, Angela, and Clint would have flown down from Montana with their son if there had been time. Everyone else was there. That was just the way this family did things. That solidarity and strength was what made them wonderful.

And formidable. She wondered if Chance Adams had any idea what a united front he was about to go up against.

Maritza had reacted to the sudden dinner party with her usual aplomb. The table was filled with platters of the black-bean burritos, the chicken enchiladas and savory beef tacos that everyone loved. There were huge bowls of *pico de gallo* and hot sauce spicy enough to burn the roof of your mouth.

To Jenny's amazement, her father remained absolutely quiet about the reason for the gathering until after Maritza had served the cooling caramel-topped flan for dessert. Maybe he'd figured digesting all that Mexican food was going to be difficult enough without mixing in stress.

Or maybe he was just putting off the bad news

because he feared getting into it at all. Jenny observed him intently all during the meal and noticed he barely touched his food, even though it was something he loved and rarely got a chance to eat since Maritza had taken to keeping a close eye on his diet. Whatever had happened years ago with this long-lost brother was clearly eating away at him now.

"I suppose you're wondering why I insisted on getting all of you together in such a hurry," he began, silencing the small talk and good-natured bickering going on around the table. He cleared his throat. "Something's come up and I felt it couldn't wait till Sunday."

Everyone's expression sobered at once.

"You're not sick, are you, Daddy?" Luke asked worriedly. "You look a little pale."

"Just sick at heart," Harlan said. "Like I said, something's happened and it concerns all of you. You have a right to know what's going on."

Luke exchanged a look with Cody and Jordan. "Whatever it is, Daddy, you can count on us. You know that," Luke said.

"Agreed," the other brothers chimed in.

"You may not be so quick to side with me once you've heard the whole story."

"What story, Grandpa Harlan?" Justin asked.

Jenny watched her father draw a deep breath before he began.

"It all started a long time ago," he said, "around the time I married your grandma Mary." He shook his head as if to clear it, then continued, "No, it began longer ago than that. You see, I had a brother back then, a brother named Henry. Everyone around here called him Hank." He smiled ruefully. "And a lot worse from time to time."

"My God," Jordan's daughter, Dani, murmured, looking shocked. "Betty Lou told me about him months ago when I was out there treating her dog after that hit-and-run. Remember, Duke? You were with me."

"I remember," her new husband said.

Jenny stared at her. "You knew? Why didn't you say anything?"

Dani shrugged. "I meant to, but..." She glanced at her husband and smiled ruefully. "Let's just say a lot of things happened. Anyway, I'd forgotten all about it, partly because I just thought she was mixed up."

"And partly because you and Duke couldn't keep your eyes off each other," Justin taunted his sister.

"Enough, son," Jordan said. "Let's hear what your grandfather has to say."

"I'm afraid Betty Lou was right," Harlan said. "Hank was very real and a handsome enough scoundrel that I'm sure quite a few ladies around town would remember him well."

"Didn't you and Hank get along, Grandpa Harlan?" Justin wanted to know.

Harlan sighed and his expression turned faintly nostalgic. "When we were boys, I suppose we got along well enough, though I was much older. Maybe that was the problem. I didn't pay enough attention when he started getting into trouble. It was little things at first. Shopkeepers would complain to Mama that he was taking a pack of gum or a candy bar. Folks around town caught him smoking when he was barely into his teens."

Justin and Harlan Patrick exchanged guilty glances. Cody scowled at them. "You two will explain those looks later," he said. "Go on, Daddy."

"Then Mama and Daddy died. I was twenty-five, a newlywed. I didn't have time for a brother who was getting into a mess of trouble every time I turned around. Petty thievery got worse. I bailed him out time and time again, feeling guilty because I hadn't tried to stop his mischief."

He paused and rubbed his eyes. To Jenny's shock it almost looked as if he'd been about to cry. She'd rarely seen him this emotional, except perhaps on the day Lizzy had been born.

"Now that I think back," he said, "I suppose his behavior was a cry for attention, but at the time I just wanted him out of my life. I was ashamed of him. I was struggling to get this place back on its feet, and for every step I'd take forward, he'd do something to pull me right back into debt. I was either paying off court costs or paying off neighbors not to press charges."

"Maybe you should have left him in jail a time or two," Jordan said, eyeing his own son in a way that had Justin squirming.

"Maybe I should have," her father conceded. "I couldn't do it."

"What did you do?"

"I sent him away. Actually I got the judge to release him from jail one last time on the condition he would leave West Texas. I gave him some money, enough of a stake to start over someplace, and told him to get out of Los Piños and not come back, that there was nothing for him here—no home, no family. I was cruel."

"He sounds like he was no good, Daddy. You just did what you had to do," Cody said loyally.

"He was my brother," Harlan said fiercely. "That should have counted for something, just the way I've always taught all of you to stick by one another through thick and thin. I failed him."

"He went, then? And stayed away?" Luke asked.

"Oh, yes, he went," Harlan said with little satisfaction. "He stole a piece of valuable antique jewelry, a ruby-and-diamond pin, on his way out the door, but he went."

"And you never heard from again?" Jenny asked.

"Not so much as a whisper—until now," the old man said wearily. "I didn't know if he was dead or alive."

"You never looked for him?" Jenny asked.

"Never. I told myself it was for the best to leave things as they were."

"Will you tell Chance the whole story?" she asked. She doubted Chance had ever heard this particular version from his own father.

Harlan sighed. "Only if I have to. It's not the kind of story a man should have to hear about his father. Could be Hank lived an exemplary life from the day he left. If he did, it would be a shame to ruin that memory for his son."

Jenny thought of the bitter, determined man she'd met the day before. He was hell-bent on revenge and enjoying the prospect. He'd never accept platitudes or evasive answers. Eventually Harlan would have to tell him everything. There wasn't a doubt in her mind about that. The only real question was how soon the subject was likely to come up.

"Is there a chance he could make a legitimate claim against White Pines?" Cody asked, looking at Jenny's mother, who practiced law in town.

"Legally he might have some rights," her mother said. "I'd have to check the terms of the will."

Harlan shot a commiserating look at his youngest son. Though everyone in the family would someday own a share of White Pines, they all knew that Cody was the one who'd poured his heart and soul into the running of it. Harlan Patrick was showing every sign of wanting to follow in his daddy's and grand-daddy's footsteps.

"No need to look," Harlan said quietly. "Legally there's nothing. The deed's in my name and mine alone. My father made sure of that before he died. He'd already seen that Hank couldn't handle responsibility."

One by one Harlan seared them with a pointed look. "But every single one of you knows there's sometimes a big difference between doing what's legal and doing what's right."

Jenny watched her stepbrother's expression shift from shock to outrage. "You intend to cut him in on the property, give him his half?" Cody demanded, halfway out of his chair.

"Settle down, Cody. I didn't say that," Harlan said. "I haven't decided yet what's fair. The truth is White Pines all but belongs to the whole lot of you now. If a decision has to be made, then all of you are going to have to make it together. From what Jenny tells me, the wolf is only a few miles from the doorstep. I just wanted you to have all the facts before you reach a conclusion about how to face him."

"You're dumping this into our laps?" Cody asked, his expression incredulous. "Is that what you're saying?"

Jenny regarded her father intently. Suddenly he was looking surprisingly pleased with himself.

"That's what I'm saying," he said.

"Well, I'll be damned," Luke murmured. He grinned at his father. "You're a sly old fox, you know that? Not many men get a whopper of a test like this to see how well they've raised their offspring."

Jenny glanced from one to the other and concluded that Luke had it exactly right. Her father intended to use Chance Adams's threat as a test of some kind to see what the rest of them were made of.

What she couldn't quite figure out, though, was whether he wanted to see them fight to keep White Pines intact or if he wanted them to parcel out a share to his newly discovered nephew. She wondered if he even knew himself, or if, for once in his life, her father was counting on his descendants to show him the way.

Chapter Four

Petey was on his best behavior for the remainder of that first week of school. Chance knew it, because there was no sign of Miss Prim and Prissy on his doorstep. He was forced to admit to being just a little disappointed.

Jenny Adams hadn't been out of his mind for more than a few minutes at a time since they'd met. He wasn't crazy about that fact, but he was honest enough to admit that on some level he'd enjoyed their brief sparring match.

Fortunately for him it wasn't in Petey's nature to stay reformed for long. On Tuesday of the following week there she was again, her face set in a disapproving scowl, her lush lips turned down in a frown and a contradictory blush in her cheeks that Chance suspected had very little to do with addressing his son's sins. Damn, but Ms. Jenny Adams was cute, a description she would no doubt hate.

"Lost control again, did you?" he inquired lightly when she marched down the driveway to stand toe-to-toe with him.

"Three generals and the entire marine corps couldn't control your son," she declared.

Chance hid a grin at her confession. He liked a woman who could admit she didn't have all the answers. He regarded her sympathetically. "Then you see what I'm up against."

She shot a look at Petey, who was regarding them warily, as if they were the last two people on earth in whom he'd want to entrust his life. Chance decided his son didn't need to observe the upcoming negotiations over his fate.

He sent Petey inside with strict instructions to go straight to his room. "No TV," he added, more for effect than any chance the punishment would be followed. Petey would probably have the remote control in hand before the words were out of his father's mouth.

When he was gone, Chance cut straight to the topic that was uppermost in his mind, though clearly not in hers. If he could distract her from Petey's misbehavior for a minute or two, so much the better.

"So, did you pass on the word regarding my intent to get my hands on White Pines?" he asked.

Her frown deepened at the question. "I'm not

your messenger,'' she retorted without missing a beat.

He grinned at the evasion. "No, but you strike me as a dutiful daughter. My bet is you served up the news right along with supper that night. How'd it go over? Did your daddy confirm that I was telling the truth? Did he admit he stole my father's share of the ranch right out from under him?''

The telltale color climbed in her cheeks. It was enough of an admission to suit him. She was still scowling, too, another confirmation of his guesswork. She could fib and evade all she wanted, but he knew the truth.

"Are you deliberately trying to get me to run interference for you?" she inquired testily, deliberately skirting the specifics of his questions. "Forget it, Mr. Adams. Do your own dirty work.''

Actually he had wanted to be the one to drop the bombshell in person, but events the last time he and Jenny Adams met had spun out of control too quickly. He'd blurted out the truth before he could stop himself. After that, there'd been no taking it back. He'd just spent the past few days waiting with more than a little impatience to see how events would unfold.

He'd been a little surprised that half the Adams men hadn't dropped by in the days since to tear a strip out of his hide or warn him off or maybe try to convince Wilkie to fire him and send him packing. When none of that happened, he'd been almost disappointed. The possibility that they'd simply dismissed his threat as nonsense hadn't even occurred to him until now.

His gaze narrowed. "Did I get it wrong? Did your father call me a liar? Is that what happened?" he asked. "Did he claim he'd never had a brother?"

She regarded him with exasperation. "Mr. Adams, I told you before—this is something you're going to have to take up personally with my father."

Her refusal to use his first name, her refusal to get involved, irritated him more than it should have. His fight was with Harlan Adams. At the moment, though, he was a whole lot more interested in sparring with the woman standing before him. Obviously that perverse streak of his where she was concerned hadn't gone away. He deliberately locked gazes with her.

"Chance," he instructed softly. More experienced women than Miss Prim and Prissy had come unglued under that direct gaze of his. As he'd expected, she swallowed hard and blinked.

"What?" she murmured, looking a little dazed.

"My name is Chance."

As if she needed to clear her head, she shook it, but she stubbornly refused to give in to his desire to hear his name on her lips. Because he couldn't help himself, he reached out and brushed the pad of his thumb across her lower lip. She trembled at the touch—but so did he. In fact, nothing had shaken him so badly in years. Reacting to Jenny Adams, except for the sheer perverse fun of it, was not a complication he could tolerate.

As a result he was suddenly all too eager to see the last of her. He told himself he'd simply tired of the game, but the truth was she was a potential distraction he didn't need. He'd just realized exactly how dangerous she was to his equilibrium and to his plan.

He allowed himself one last caress of her silken cheek, lingered long enough to feel her skin heat beneath his touch, then withdrew with regret. Confusion and desire were at odds in her flashing eyes. He knew just how she felt. Her expression mirrored his own unexpectedly jittery reaction.

"I've got work to do," he announced abruptly. "Maybe you ought to get to the point of this visit."

The chill in his voice seemed to startle her. "It's, um…" She cleared her throat. "It's Petey."

"I assumed that much."

"He's not paying attention in class."

"Maybe you should make the lessons more interesting," he suggested, enjoying the fresh flood of color in her cheeks. He didn't want Petey challenging his teacher's authority, but that didn't mean Chance couldn't take pleasure in it.

"Mister Adams," she said, drawing it out and using that prim and prissy tone he found so irritating.

"Chance," he corrected again.

"I think I see where your son gets his problems with authority," she retorted.

Chance chuckled. He didn't intend to mention that he'd very firmly instructed his son that he was to show respect for this particular authority figure. He held up his hands.

"Okay, I'm sorry," he apologized. "I know you have a tough job. Tell me what Petey has done to make it more difficult. You said he wasn't paying attention in class. I assume there's more to it."

"There is. If he was reading a book or staring out the window, it would be one thing. Only his grades would suffer. But it's worse than that. He's deliberately distracting the others, drawing them into his mischief. He ignores any attempt I make to silence him. He's setting a terrible example for his classmates. Have you ever considered having him tested for ADD? That's attention deficit disorder."

Chance stared at her, torn between incredulity and outrage. "I know what it is, Ms. Adams. ADD is not Petey's problem. If you've looked at his school records, then you must be aware that he's a very bright boy."

"Many ADD kids are."

"He's received exemplary report cards. Mostly *A*'s and *B*'s. He was never a problem student in any way, shape or form back in Montana. No detentions, no suspensions." Chance regarded her evenly. "I guess that brings us back to you."

She sighed and a little of the spunk seemed to drain out of her. "I was afraid you were going to say that. Maybe I really am no good at this."

Chance was startled by the abrupt turnaround. "You're not giving up, are you?"

"A good teacher would know how to cope with

one troubled nine-year-old boy," she said, her expression bleak.

"Petey's not troubled," Chance insisted.

"Of course he is. He's suffered two devastating losses in the last couple of years. Obviously they've taken a toll. He's lashing out at me. I understand that, I really do, but I have no idea what to do about it."

Chance sighed. "He's not lashing out at you because of anything you're doing or not doing," he said. "He's lashing out because of who you are."

She absorbed his statement, then slowly nodded. "An Adams," she concluded. "Of course."

"Exactly. I've told him he was not to let this dispute I have to settle with your father spill over into the classroom, but he's a kid and he's very loyal to his grandfather. He worshiped the old coot and he took to heart all the animosity my father had for Harlan Adams. Now, rightly or wrongly, that hatred extends to you."

"And you've encouraged that, too, I'm sure."

"Just by coming here I suppose I have, but believe me, I did not intend for you to suffer any fallout. I have a lot of respect for teachers. I never meant to make your job more difficult. My problem's with your father, not you."

Jenny sighed again and sank onto the stump he'd been using the week before as a chopping block. When she gazed up at him with those huge, despairing eyes, his stomach turned flip-flops.

"What are we going to do about this mess?" she

asked. "There's nothing I can do about being Harlan Adams's daughter. I wouldn't even if I could. I'm very proud of it."

Chance found he liked this softer more vulnerable side to her almost as much as he enjoyed the sass and vinegar. "You mean to tell me you don't have all the answers?"

"Not half of them," she conceded.

Chance was struck by an inspiration. Of course, it was just the teensiest bit self-serving, but so what? The point was to get Petey to behave in school. His son needed to stop thinking of Jenny Adams as the enemy, right?

"Go out with me," he suggested impulsively. At her stunned expression, he promptly amended the idea. "I meant with us. To dinner. Petey's been dying to try that Italian restaurant in town. We could all go. He's basically a friendly, loving kid. If he sees I'm not treating you like a bad guy, maybe he'll get the message. I've told him of course, but actions speak louder than words."

"Has it also occurred to you that this could backfire? Maybe he'll conclude that means I'll give him good grades just because you and I are friends."

Chance grinned. "Yeah, but you're tougher than that, so it's not a problem. A couple of *F*'s and he should get the message."

Jenny regarded him skeptically. "We're talking one dinner here, right? Just a pleasant evening so Petey can get to know me informally and conclude

I'm an okay person, maybe separate me from the feud with my father.''

"Exactly."

"There's a flaw in here somewhere, but for the life of me I can't figure out what it is. Besides, I'm a desperate woman. I'll try anything."

Chance wasn't exactly crazy about the implication that only a desperate woman would be willing to have dinner with him, but he was too relieved by the acceptance to bother questioning the reasoning behind it. As for his own logic in asking, that didn't bear any scrutiny at all. Not ten minutes earlier he'd been warning himself to stay the hell away from her.

"Do you want to go now or do you need to go home first?" he asked.

"Now is fine. Except for Petey, it was actually one of the better days at school. No one threw food or paint, so I'm still looking halfway respectable."

Chance took a lazy, deliberate survey from head to toe and nodded. "More than halfway," he said approvingly. "I'll get Petey."

To his annoyance Petey was less than enthusiastic about the plan, despite the promise of pizza.

"I'm not going," he declared, folding his arms across his little chest and glaring up at Chance.

"Excuse me?"

"I'm not," Petey repeated.

"Oh, but you are," Chance countered. "You have exactly five seconds to get those shoes on and that shirt tucked in." He studied his son more carefully. "And another sixty seconds to get in the bathroom and wash your face."

Petey wasted a good many of those seconds glaring back at his father. Chance returned the gaze evenly and slowly started counting. Finally Petey jammed his feet into his sneakers without bothering to untie them and stomped off to the bathroom. Chance considered it a small victory.

When Petey returned, his face was scrubbed clean and even his hair was combed more neatly. He looked up into Chance's eyes. "I just don't get it, Dad. Why are you being so nice to her? What do you care if she hates our guts now or after we take back White Pines?"

"Because none of this is her fault," Chance said. "Harlan Adams adopted her when she was only a little older than you are now. Why blame her for something he did years and years before that?"

Petey stared at Chance incredulously. "You sound like you even like her a little bit. You don't, do you, Dad? I mean not like a guy likes a girl or something."

"No, of course not," Chance said a little too quickly. Anyone with the least bit of understanding of the battle of the sexes would have seen straight through the sharp denial. Fortunately, as bright as he was, Petey wasn't savvy enough to guess the truth—that Chance was growing more intrigued with Jenny Adams by the minute.

Before all was said and done, he had a feeling one of them was going to be hurt. Given his avowed mission in Los Piños, it was clear to him which one of them it was going to be.

Before he could suffer too many pangs of regret over that, Petey's expression brightened.

"Hey, I get it," he said. "You're, like, sneaking into the enemy camp. You're gonna use Ms. Adams to find out what's going on with her dad, huh?"

Chance didn't want to acknowledge that the very same reprehensible idea had occurred to him. It sounded so low-down and sleazy when Petey said it that he found himself denying the possibility.

"Son, we're going to dinner, nothing more. You've been wanting to try the Italian place to see what their pizza's like. I figured it wouldn't hurt to have some feminine company so we don't forget our table manners."

"Yeah, sure."

"That's all," Chance insisted.

Petey shot him a look of pure disgust, either because he didn't like the idea of Ms. Adams telling him which fork to use or because he'd concluded that Chance was a very bad liar. Either way it appeared they were in for an interesting dinner.

Jenny should have known better than to accept Chance's invitation. Oh, sure, his intentions were probably honorable enough. They both wanted to improve her relationship with Petey so they could survive the school year.

But agreeing to go to the Italian restaurant in town was as much as begging for trouble. Half her relatives showed up there for meals at least once a week. With as many relatives as she had, she and Chance were pretty much destined to run into somebody from the family.

Thankfully it was Dani and Duke tonight, she thought as she hurriedly surveyed the crowded tables from the doorway. Those two were still so besotted with each other maybe neither of them would notice her. The twins weren't with them, either, so they were busy gazing into each other's eyes. Maybe they wouldn't waste this rare night out alone by sticking their noses into Jenny's business.

"That booth in the corner is open," Jenny said, practically bolting for it before Chance could choose another table. She slid in so that her back was toward Dani and Duke. When she was settled snugly into a corner, she glanced up into Chance's amused eyes.

"Hiding from someone you know?"

She couldn't think of a good reason not to tell him the truth. In a town the size of Los Piños, sooner or later he would get to know the whole family whether he made good on his threat to go after White Pines or not.

"My niece, actually. My stepbrother Jordan's adopted daughter. She's the town vet. She just married Duke Jenkins. He works for her father's oil company."

"How cozy," Chance said with a surprising touch of sarcasm. "Any particular reason you're trying to avoid them?"

Jenny swallowed hard and admitted, "I'm not exactly sure how I'd explain this."

"You mean being here with Petey and me?"

She nodded.

"How about the truth? I asked. You said yes."

"It's more complicated than that and you know it."

Petey sat patiently enough through most of their conversation, but judging from his expression, he'd finally tired of it. "Are we ever gonna eat?" he asked.

Jenny smiled at him. "Right now in fact. I'm starved," she confided. "And this place has the very best pizza I've ever tasted."

"Not as good as we used to get back in Montana, I'll bet," Petey declared.

"Better even than what I used to get in New York City," she countered. "What do you like on yours?"

He directed a belligerent look at her and said, "Anchovies."

Jenny managed not to gag. Instead, she beamed back at him. "Me, too."

Chance chuckled. "Okay, son, now what?"

Jenny regarded Petey innocently. "You mean you don't really like anchovies?"

Petey sighed heavily. "Not really." He eyed her warily. "Do you? Are we gonna have to get 'em?"

"No, I can live without anchovies this once. How about pepperoni, instead?"

"And sausage," Petey added.

She glanced over at Chance. "Okay with you?"

"Hey, I'm at your mercy. Whatever you two decide."

Jenny grinned. "Then pepperoni and sausage it is."

The harried waitress, Maria, finally rushed over to take their order. "I don't know what's going on in here tonight. It's the middle of the week and every table's taken. Doesn't anybody cook at home anymore?"

"I'm the wrong person to ask," Jenny said. "From the moment I left New York years ago, I've been suffering withdrawal symptoms from the lack of takeout. Until I came here at fourteen I thought that was how dinner was served in most homes. Chinese takeout was my favorite and I had at least a half-dozen restaurants in the neighborhood to choose from."

"Don't tell Maritza that," Maria said. "She'll go on strike out at White Pines if she thinks you'd rather have Chinese takeout than her home cooking."

Jenny held up her hands. "No, no, don't misunderstand. Maritza was my salvation. If it had been up to my mom, we'd have lived on burned toast and tuna salad with an occasional boiled egg tossed in. And before Mom married Harlan, I'd have starved if it hadn't been for this place." She glanced at Petey and explained, "My mother is a truly terrible cook. Maritza, the housekeeper at White Pines, cringes whenever Mom comes near the kitchen. She shoos her right back out again.''

''Hey, that sounds like dad,'' Petey said.

''Watch it, kid,'' Chance warned.

''Your dad's not a very good cook?'' Jenny asked, amused by this bit of information. Chance Adams had struck her as the kind of man who'd be very very good at whatever he put his mind to.

''If it doesn't come frozen, we don't eat it,'' Petey said.

''That's not true,'' Chance said indignantly. ''I can open cans, too.''

The waitress grinned. ''Well, you're in for a treat tonight, then. The food here's the best in town. I highly recommend the pizza and the lasagna. The lasagna's my mom's old family recipe from Italy.'' She looked at Jenny. ''Hey, did you see Dani and Duke on your way in? Want me to tell 'em you're here?''

''No, that's okay. They think they're still on their honeymoon. Let 'em pretend a while longer.''

When the waitress had left, Chance regarded her quizzically. ''Honeymoon? When were they married?''

''Right after Valentine's Day.''

''That's more than six months ago.''

''But they only get about fifteen minutes a week alone. Duke has twin boys and a high-pressure job that takes him out of town from time to time. Dani's a vet. She gets calls at all hours of the night.''

"Ah, I see. Exactly how many people are we talking about in your family?"

"It depends on whether you count all of us who've been adopted in or married in."

"Let's say I do."

"Okay, there would be Harlan and my mother, me and my half sister, Lizzy. Lizzy's the baby. Then there are my three older stepbrothers and their wives, Dani and Duke, Sharon Lynn and her fiancé, Justin and Harlan Patrick, Angela and Clint, plus Duke's boys and Angie and Clint's baby. You do the math."

She shot him a belligerent look. "And no matter where we actually live, we all consider White Pines home."

Chance chuckled. "Is that supposed to be a warning, darlin'?"

"They do say there's strength in numbers, but you take it any way you like."

"I think I'll just consider it a challenge, then." He glanced past her shoulder. "And don't look now, but we're about to have company. Get ready to do some explaining."

Jenny bit back a sigh and turned to watch Dani and Duke approach.

"We're just on our way out," Dani said, leaning down to give Jenny a kiss on the cheek. "We stopped by to say hi." She regarded Chance curiously. "Hi. We haven't met."

"Dani and Duke, this is Chance Adams," Jenny said with reluctance. "And his son, Petey."

Dani's extended hand halted in midair and her

expression froze. "Mr. Adams," she said with a curt nod.

The chilliness in her voice startled Jenny. She'd never known Dani to be impolite to anyone.

"Mrs. Jenkins," Chance said quietly, ignoring the snub. He shook Duke's hand as if he hadn't even noticed that Dani's had been withdrawn. "A pleasure to meet you both."

"Same here," Duke said, his tone neutral.

Dani turned a speculative gaze on Jenny. "We'll talk tomorrow. How about Dolan's at four-thirty?"

There was no question it was a command performance for Dani and Sharon Lynn, who ran the place. Jenny could have wriggled off the hook, but it would only have been delaying the inevitable. If she didn't show up, Dani and Sharon Lynn would probably invade her classroom at midday and demand answers.

"I'll do my best to make it," she said.

Dani did grin ever so slightly at that. "Yes, I imagine you will."

"Good night," Duke said, giving Jenny's shoulder a supportive squeeze. He leaned down to whisper, "Give 'em hell, kiddo."

Jenny wasn't exactly sure whether he'd misinterpreted her presence here with Chance as an infiltration of the enemy camp or whether he was referring to her upcoming meeting with his wife and Sharon Lynn. She managed a halfhearted smile in response.

After they'd gone Chance regarded her intently. "I gather you're not looking forward to this little get-together tomorrow."

"Hardly. If I was an evil person, I'd insist you go in my place," she said in a dire tone. "You're the one with the answers they really want."

"I could join you," he offered readily. "It might be interesting."

Jenny tried to imagine her nieces' reaction to that and concluded she was better off facing them alone. "Never mind," she said wearily. "I know enough of their secrets to keep them in line."

"Oh, really?" Chance said, obviously fascinated. "Care to share?"

"Not on your life. If you intend to blackmail this family, you'll have to find your own means to do it."

"There'll be no blackmail, darlin'. Sooner or later I'll just claim what's rightfully mine."

"Yeah," Petey chimed in. "Nobody's going to stop us."

Jenny admired their confidence if not their intentions. "Simple as that, huh?"

"Simple as that," Chance concurred.

Jenny shook her head and thought of the formidable lineup of foes he faced. "You poor deluded man."

Rather than taking offense, he smiled. "We'll see."

Something in his tone raised the hairs on her arms. For the briefest of instants she wondered if she hadn't been a little too quick to dismiss him. Chance Adams suddenly struck her as an astonishingly formidable force himself.

Chapter Five

As things turned out, Chance was glad he'd persuaded Jenny to leave her car at his place when they
came into town for dinner. If he hadn't, he was very
much afraid she would have bolted from the dinner
table after the encounter with Duke and Dani Jenkins.

Whether Jenny cared to admit it or not, she had
been deeply shaken by her niece's reaction to finding the two of them together. Even though she had
clearly expected it, had even tried to prevent their
being seen, Dani's shocked response to the intro-
duction to Harlan's avowed enemy had taken Jenny
by surprise.

He could understand her worry, could even sym-
pathize with it on an objective level. No doubt she

had felt like a traitor. Chance wondered if her father would consider her one, as well, when he learned of the dinner they'd shared.

"How's Harlan going to react when he finds out we were out together?" he asked, drawing a startled look.

Jenny had been concentrating very hard on the slice of pizza she'd been toying with for the past few minutes. She hadn't swallowed more than a couple of bites. Petey, oblivious to the tension and the undercurrents, had been gobbling up more than his share.

"I'm not sure," she confessed, her expression bleak. "I mean, it's not a big deal, right? It's dinner."

"That would certainly be the tack I'd take," he said, deliberately insinuating there were other less innocuous explanations.

She stared at him. "Meaning?"

He regarded her with pure innocence. "Meaning that I'd kiss it off as a simple uncomplicated meal. Who could make anything out of that?"

"It *is* an innocent meal."

"If you say so. Obviously, though, your niece didn't think so. Whose version do you think the rest of the family will believe? My hunch is they're all prepared to think the worst of me."

Clearly agitated by the question, she glanced at Petey, dug in her purse and handed him a handful of quarters. "There are some video games in that alcove over there. Why don't you go try them?"

"I'm not finished eating," Petey protested.

"Please," Jenny said.

When Petey glanced at him, Chance knew Petey was hoping for a reprieve. Instead, he gestured toward the games. "Go. You know you love video games."

Pete's turned-down mouth indicated his displeasure, but he slid out of the booth. "Okay, but you'd better leave the last slice of pizza for me," he warned. "I've only had two and I'm still hungry."

"You've had three, but you'll get another piece," Chance promised, eager to send him on his way and see just what Jenny had on her mind. "And thank Ms. Adams for the change."

"Yeah, sure," he grumbled ungraciously. "Thanks."

When Petey was gone, Chance directed a solemn look at the woman across the table. "I take it you had something you wanted to say in private."

She lifted her gaze and met his evenly. "I just wanted to make sure we were clear about something."

"What's that?"

"You and I..." She waved her hand dismissively as if no other words were necessary.

Chance got the message, but he wanted her to spell it out just the same. "Yes?" he prodded.

"There is no you and I, no us, no anything, correct? We established that before we ever left your house."

She was so darned determined to tidy up the situation, to establish the limits of their friendship, that he couldn't help giving her a difficult time. He returned her look with a perfectly bland expression. "If you say so, darlin'."

"I do," she said firmly.

Chance grinned. "Last time I heard those two words said with so much passion I was standing in a church."

She scowled at him. "Chance!"

"Yes, darlin'?"

She sighed heavily. "Oh, never mind."

"Tell me. You can tell me anything, you know."

"And you'll find a way to use it against my father, no doubt."

"Not all my motives are ulterior. In fact, I think I'm developing a case of straightforward lust where you're concerned."

She frowned, creating an endearing little furrow between her brows. He wanted to kiss it away.

"Blast it, Chance!" she said. "Stop looking at me like that and stop saying things like that. This situation is complicated enough without you suggesting that there's some sort of chemistry between us."

"There is," he said. "It might be a tad inconvenient under the circumstances, but life is messy. I've learned it's best to go with the flow."

She regarded him incredulously. "Oh, really. You don't strike me as a go-with-the-flow kind of guy. Not many men who claim to be hell-bent on revenge would even try to pass themselves off as laid-back."

He shrugged. "Contradictions are a part of life."

"Oh, save your dime-store philosophy. This dinner was about me trying to get Petey's respect so he'll settle down in class. That's absolutely all it was about. I would never have agreed to it otherwise."

"Maybe for you that's all it was," he taunted, and allowed his own interpretation to remain unspoken. In fact, Chance was enjoying himself too much to stop teasing her now. Besides, there was more than a little truth behind his taunts. He could easily get addicted to watching that blossoming of pink in her cheeks, that rise of indignation that darkened her eyes. He sat back and enjoyed the predictable return of both.

She leaped to her feet, then leaned across the table until she was in his face.

"Stop that this instant," she demanded.

Chance couldn't help himself. He chuckled. Big mistake. Her eyes flashed with pure fire. It was a little like staring into a bed of flaming coals. It was downright mesmerizing.

"Damn you, Chance Adams!" she shouted, oblivious to the stares she was drawing.

Aware that she intended to say a whole lot more at full volume, he stood up, too, a move that forced her to take a quick step back until the booth's bench caught the back of her knees and trapped her where she was. Even though the table still separated them, he could feel the heat radiating from every furious fiber of her being.

He reached over and cupped her face in his hands,

then murmured only half apologetically, "Darlin', this is for your own good."

Before she could guess his intentions, he kissed her. The position was awkward, the stares disconcerting, the table an impossible barrier, but Chance gave his all to that kiss. The instant his lips touched hers, all that mattered was the wildfire it set off in his veins and making sure it never stopped.

Jenny trembled, quite possibly with fury. He was quaking for another reason entirely. The sensual feel of her mouth under his, the taste of her, the scent of her spicy, sexy perfume all combined to scare the daylights out of him. He'd begun by teasing, but what was happening right now, with Jenny's mouth surrendering to his, was deadly serious. He backed off as if he'd inadvertently touched an open flame.

Jenny remained exactly where he'd left her, hands braced on the table, eyes dazed. When she realized he'd released her, she sank back onto the bench as if her knees would no longer support her. She stared at him, blinked several times, then ran her tongue slowly over her lips.

That last unthinking gesture almost cost Chance his very fragile grip on sanity. If she'd done it again, he might have picked her up caveman-style and carried her out of the restaurant and off to the nearest bed...or floor...or hayloft.

"What...?" She began, but her voice trailed off. She swallowed hard and tried again. "Why...?"

Chance searched for any explanation besides the truth. He wasn't about to admit he'd impulsively and thoroughly kissed her solely because he'd no longer been able to resist. In fact, he dimly recalled that there'd been another reason entirely at the outset.

"You were about to cause a scene," he said, remembering. "I figured it would be better if people thought it was a lovers' tiff."

"Why?"

For one halfway honorable instant, he'd had some crazy notion about protecting her reputation, but he supposed a case could be made that the very public kiss hadn't done much for that, either. In fact, when the truth came out about the reason he'd come to Los Piños, more folks than Dani Jenkins would be labeling Jenny a traitor, especially if they'd seen that kiss. Unexpected guilt made him edgy, so he skirted the truth with lighthearted banter.

"I'm an impulsive man. It seemed like the right thing to do at the time."

"Impulsive? Go with the flow?" Her skepticism was plain in her tone and in her expression. "These are not words I would use to describe you," she said.

"Maybe you just don't know me all that well."

"No," she conceded, "I probably don't, but some things it doesn't take more than a few minutes to figure out."

He regarded her speculatively. "We could work on changing that so you know the real me, all of it."

Alarm flared in her eyes. "Oh, no. No way.

You're not dragging me into the middle of this mess. It's complicated enough already.''

"You're already in the middle," he pointed out.

"No, I'm not. I'm Harlan Adams's daughter, period.''

"And my son's teacher.''

"That part's not a problem," she claimed.

"That part is what brought us here tonight," he reminded her.

"Well, it won't happen again, that's all. Either Petey learns to behave in class or..." Her voice trailed off.

He wasn't crazy about that unspoken threat. "Or what?" he demanded quietly.

Her chin jutted. Her gaze clashed with his. "Or I'll see he's suspended.''

The threat, about what he'd expected, had Chance's hackles rising. "And I'll tell the principal you're taking your displeasure with me out on my son.'' Chance kept his tone even and friendly, but he was pretty sure she got the message he was seething.

"That's blackmail," she accused, clearly not the least bit intimidated.

"If you're going to use that label for me, I might as well live up to it. Besides, I call it protecting my boy. You don't want to be caught in the middle. I don't want him to be caught in the middle. I'd say we're at an impasse.''

"Why don't you just come out to White Pines,

have it out with my father and get it over with?"
she asked a little plaintively.

It was an approach Chance had considered and
then dismissed. He shrugged. "Too easy. I figure I
ought to let you all stew for a while wondering when
I'll make my move and what form it'll take."

"Don't wait too long," she warned in a somber
tone. "My father's in his eighties. He's got a softer,
more forgiving heart than the rest of us. You'd do
better to make peace with him than to wait around
and risk having to deal with his sons and daughters.
And if there's so much as a hint that stress was
behind something happening to him, there'd be hell
to pay."

Chance thought about that grim warning long after he'd taken Jenny back to her car and watched
her drive away. The only problem was, he didn't
want to make peace with Harlan Adams. He'd become more and more dedicated to making him pay
for what he'd done to his younger brother. Chance
wanted him to suffer during whatever time he had
left here on earth, and then he wanted him to rot in
hell. White Pines might not hold the same mystique
for Chance that it had for his father, but getting his
hands on it was the least he owed Hank.

Jenny would have preferred being pilloried to
walking into Dolan's drugstore the next afternoon to
face Sharon Lynn and Dani. Although technically
she was their stepaunt, they were close enough in
age that they'd always treated one another more like

very tight-knit cousins, maybe even sisters. Jenny had a feeling this afternoon they were going to be regarding her more like a traitor.

The irony, of course, was that going out with Chance and Petey had stirred up all this trouble and accomplished absolutely nothing. If anything, Petey had been even more impossible in class today.

As she'd feared, he seemed to think their dinner the night before implied she'd be lax in disciplining him. He'd seemed stunned when she'd hauled him out of the classroom and planted his little butt on a chair in the hall and told him to stay there and think about whether he wanted an education or if he'd prefer to go through life ignorant.

"I'm going to tell my dad about this," he'd threatened. "And he will never, ever kiss you again."

"I can live with that," Jenny had muttered, determined to ignore the terrible sinking sensation the threat stirred in the pit of her stomach. She had liked kissing Chance Adams entirely too much.

"Yeah, well, you're gonna have to," Petey shot back.

All in all it had been a rotten day. And there was more to come, she thought as she glanced around Dolan's.

At four-thirty the soda-fountain counter was mostly empty. Two teenage boys, who had a crush on the older and very out-of-their-reach Sharon Lynn, were finishing their soft drinks when Jenny came in. Dani wasn't there yet.

Jenny breathed a sigh of relief. Maybe Dani hadn't even filled Sharon Lynn in on what she'd seen the night before.

Her hopes were dashed when she saw Sharon Lynn's speculative expression. If Dani hadn't spread the word, then someone else surely had. Los Piños thrived on gossip, especially when it concerned a member of the Adams clan. Some folks in Los Piños thought the family had been born and bred purely to provide them with titillating entertainment.

"Hi," she said as she slid onto a stool. "I gather you've been expecting me."

"Dani mentioned she was meeting you here," Sharon Lynn said neutrally.

"Did she also mention why?"

"Something about you being out with Chance Adams last night."

Jenny sighed. Sharon Lynn grinned and took her sweet time pouring a soda for her.

"Of course a few other folks in town have had a far more fascinating tale to tell," Sharon Lynn said as she set the drink on the counter. "One I don't think Dani knows about yet."

"Oh?"

"The word is, he planted a kiss on you that had half the women in town swooning. True or false?"

"I can't attest to whether or not anyone swooned," Jenny said evasively.

"But he did kiss you?"

"Yes," she admitted reluctantly. "He claimed it

was to keep me from slugging him and causing a scene.''

Sharon Lynn chuckled. ''An interesting approach.'' She peered closely at Jenny. ''So how was it?''

''What?''

''The kiss?''

''Is that all you care about, that the man kissed me?'' Jenny demanded, then recalled that Sharon Lynn's own parents had been responsible for many a steamy scene right here in Dolan's. Maybe a lack of restraint and a streak of incurable romanticism ran through the lot of them.

''You have to admit it's the most interesting part of the story,'' Sharon Lynn said.

''I suppose that depends on who's telling it.''

''Are you saying you didn't enjoy it?''

Jenny considered lying and claiming that Chance's kiss hadn't affected her one way or the other. Other men had kissed her. It wasn't as if one kiss from Chance was anything special. For the past twenty hours or so she'd been trying to convince herself of precisely that. Sooner or later she was going to need someone to confide in. Sharon Lynn didn't seem to be judging her too harshly so far. Maybe she could tell her the truth and put the whole thing into perspective.

''My knees went weak,'' she admitted ruefully.

Sharon Lynn grinned. ''All right!''

Jenny studied her warily. ''Aren't you furious?''

''Why should I be?''

"Because of who he is. Goodness knows, I'm furious. It's an impossible situation."

Sharon Lynn waved off the obvious problem. "This may be the best for everyone concerned. You can mediate. You're very good at that. Ask those people on Capitol Hill you used to badger all the time."

Jenny groaned at Sharon Lynn's lack of understanding of her skills. She wasn't in the habit of making nice just to keep peace. More often than not, she was the one touching off dynamite, though not in the literal sense.

"I am not good at mediating," she corrected. "I am good at waking people up, stirring up controversy. My initial impression is that this time I've already stirred up a veritable hornets' nest."

"That would certainly be my impression, too," Dani said, slipping onto the stool next to her. She glared at Jenny. "What the heck were you thinking last night when you decided to go out with Chance Adams?"

Feeling defensive already, Jenny returned Dani's scowl with one of her own. "Not that I owe you an explanation, but I was thinking that I had an out-of-control student on my hands and that spending a little time with him and his father outside the classroom might help the situation."

"So that led to playing kissy-face with a sworn enemy of Harlan's?" Dani demanded, her expression incredulous. "Parent-teacher conferences with you must really be something."

Jenny winced, upset not so much by the pointed barb but by its implication. She had really really hoped that Dani hadn't heard about the kiss. It had happened after she'd gone, but obviously Dani had heard every steamy little detail. Of course half the people in the restaurant had probably made it their business to take a pet in to see Dani. Those who hadn't gone there had apparently stopped by Dolan's for a soda first thing this morning to fill Sharon Lynn in.

"I didn't kiss him. He kissed me," Jenny protested in self-defense. It wasn't much of an argument, but it was the only one she had.

"The way I heard it you didn't exactly shove him away," Dani countered. "Most people had the impression that you two were giving off more heat than the pizza oven."

Jenny hated fighting with someone she'd always loved like a sister. Because they weren't sisters, they'd rarely had cause for any of the usual sibling spats. Besides, Dani had always been even tempered and rational. She'd been a calming influence on Jenny's more fiery personality. Now she seemed hell-bent on inflaming it herself.

"Dammit, Dani, whether or not I kiss Chance Adams really isn't anyone's business but mine," Jenny all but shouted.

Dani faced her defiantly. "It is when it hurts the family."

"Who, pray tell, was hurt by my kissing a man?"

"Not just a man," Dani contradicted. "Chance Adams."

"Okay, okay, you two, settle down," Sharon Lynn soothed. "Fighting among ourselves won't help anything." She turned to Dani. "Does Grandpa Harlan known about this?"

"I haven't told him, but I can't speak for any of the direct witnesses or participants," Dani said. She glared at Jenny again. "If I were you, I'd fill him in before someone else does."

"That was my plan," Jenny said. "I would have last night, but he was already in bed when I got home."

Dani regarded her worriedly. "Were you that late or did he go to bed much earlier than usual?"

"It was early. Mom said he spent most of the day out riding. He was tired. He went to his room right after dinner."

"He was probably taking a last nostalgic look at the property this jerk intends to try to steal from him," Dani said. "How could you, Jenny? How could you consort with the enemy?"

"I've explained that. I'm not going to do it again. And for the record, I'm just as upset about Chance's threats as anyone else. Don't forget, a share of that property is going to be mine one day. My ancestors on my mother's side were robbed of it or land very much like it generations ago by white men."

"Maybe if you signed over your share to Chance, it would satisfy him," Dani suggested with an edge of bitterness. "Then Grandpa Harlan could stop worrying himself sick and Uncle Cody wouldn't be afraid that the ranch he loves is going to get carved up like a Thanksgiving turkey to satisfy some old grudge.''

"No," Sharon Lynn said sharply, startling them both. "Jenny shouldn't have to give up one single acre she's entitled to. We all need to stick together on this. That's what Grandpa Harlan wants. As for whether or not Jenny spends time with Chance, that's up to her. Maybe it'll be a good thing to have a spy in this man's camp.''

Jenny had had enough. First they called her a traitor. Now they wanted her to become a spy. The whole mess was rapidly getting out of hand. She slid off her stool and tossed a dollar on the counter to pay for her soda. "I am not in his camp. I am not spying. I am going home.''

"Enjoy it while you can," Dani said. "Unless, of course, you figure you've got an in with the prospective new owner.''

"Dani!" Sharon Lynn protested.

"Well, I can't help it. I agree with you that we should all stick together and present a united front, so cozying up to Chance Adams over pizza strikes me as being pretty darned close to treason.''

Jenny sighed. "You're entitled to your opinion.'' Dani's judgment hurt her more than she'd expected. She forced a smile for Sharon Lynn. "Bye. Stop in on your way home if you have the time.''

Sharon Lynn shot a worried look at Dani, but nodded. "I think I will.''

Dani frowned at both of them. "Well, isn't that just peachy. Doesn't anybody but me see how ludicrous this budding romance is?"

"There is no romance," Jenny said impatiently. "None, zip. *Nada.*"

Dani shook her head. "Try telling that to Grandpa Harlan and see how well it flies."

Jenny intended to do just that. Her father was the only person in the family to whom she owed any explanation at all. Somehow she would have to make him see that she hadn't betrayed him last night and that she didn't intend to in the future. Harlan would believe her. He was much more reasonable than Dani.

Most of the time, Jenny thought with a sigh.

If last night had been a disaster, tonight was already showing promise of being a full-scale calamity. And like it or not, thanks to her decision to take on the fourth grade this year, instead of sticking with eighth-grade history, she was smack-dab in the middle of it.

Chapter Six

Jenny was so distracted when she walked out of Dolan's she slammed right into what felt like a brick wall. The unexpected encounter rocked her back on her heels. Large callused hands clamped her arms to keep her upright. She promptly felt the sizzle of the contact right down to her toes.

In fact, that sizzle was her first clue to the identity of the solid wall of muscle she'd run into. Only one man had ever made such a devastating impact on her senses with little more than a touch: Chance Adams.

Her startled gaze flew up and clashed with his. He seemed amused. Come to think of it, he usually did around her, which was darned irritating. She had not been put on this earth to provide him with entertainment. Obviously Petey hadn't reported in yet about being banished to the hall, or Chance's mood wouldn't be quite so lighthearted.

"What are you doing here?" she demanded, taking her annoyance with Dani and Sharon Lynn out on him. It was his fault she'd fought with them in the first place. And the timing of his arrival today struck her as particularly suspicious. He probably intended to add to the impression that they were newly inseparable, thereby widening the rift between her and her family.

"It's a public sidewalk," he said blandly.

"And you just happened to be strolling by at this precise moment?"

"It is possible, you know."

She shook her head. "No way. I don't believe it."

"If you don't believe in coincidence, what do you think I'm doing here?"

"You came by intentionally because you knew I was going to be here with Dani and Sharon Lynn," she accused. "Even though I specifically told you to stay away."

"Why would I want to do that?" he asked.

A baby couldn't have looked more innocent. Jenny wasn't buying his act for a second.

"To stir up trouble," she said flatly.

He gestured toward the drugstore. "Is that what happened in there? The three of you had a fight?"

Still stinging from her nieces' verbal assault, she admitted, "Actually it was primarily the two of us, me and Dani. Sharon Lynn pretty much tried to mediate, but it was a lost cause. Dani's got her dander up. There's no one on earth fiercer than an Adams who's all riled up.''

''I'm sorry.''

The soft-spoken, sincere-sounding apology was the last thing she'd expected. She stared into his eyes and thought she recognized a genuine flash of sympathy.

''Are you really?'' she asked, unable to hide her skepticism. He was probably getting exactly the results he wanted: chaos in the Adams ranks.

''Yes,'' he replied emphatically. ''Believe it or not, family is every bit as important to me as it is to you. After all, why would I waste my time coming here to settle an old score between my father and his brother if it wasn't? I'd never seen White Pines. I'd never met your father. It wasn't my grudge to start with. It was my father's. He asked me to come here on his deathbed.''

''You would never have come here on your own?'' Jenny asked skeptically. ''Are you sure about that?''

''Nope. This was all my father's idea.'' His expression turned vaguely rueful. ''As a matter of fact, he manipulated me into it. He pulled out all the stops, including filling Petey's head with tales of his ancestors and the way both Petey and I had been cheated out of our heritage right along with him. Petey would never have forgiven me for not doing as his granddaddy asked.''

Chance regarded her evenly. ''It wasn't until I got

here that I turned it into my own battle. I suppose I'd always thought Daddy was exaggerating about what had been taken from him. Once I saw White Pines and heard about Harlan Adams and his power, I realized Daddy's bitterness was justified.''

Jenny could have enlightened him a bit on that point, but she figured that was her father's story to tell if he ever chose to.

"Okay," she said, instead. "So you're just a loyal son. That doesn't mean you're not also just a greedy bastard who saw an easy way to make a claim on some valuable land."

Chance's expression darkened and his eyes glittered dangerously. "Maybe you ought to take a minute one of these days and look at this from my perspective."

It was a reasonable suggestion, but Jenny wasn't feeling particularly reasonable. "Why would I want to do that?" she asked.

"Because my situation isn't all that different from the one you were in when you first came to town."

The mild comment startled her. Jenny thought back to that tumultuous period of her life. She'd been an angry teenager, bent on getting into trouble and resentful of every adult, especially those who were rich and powerful like the Adamses. It was so long in the past, so wildly different from her attitude now, that she'd virtually forgotten that time in her life.

She'd also thought it forgotten by everyone else

in Los Piños. Her gaze narrowed. "What do you know about that?"

Chance grinned and settled one hip against the fender of his truck. He hooked the heel of his boot on the bumper. No one on earth could have looked more at ease or more inclined to let her simmer for a bit and wonder who'd been filling his head with tales of her misadventures.

Jenny wished she could convey the same sort of calm. She suspected her churning emotions were plain on her face. She'd never been able to hide what she was feeling. Not for more than a minute, anyway.

When she'd first arrived in Los Piños at fourteen, everyone had known exactly how angry and bitter she was about her parents' divorce, about the move from New York, about the sins she felt had been committed against her Native American ancestors. All that rage had taken the form of some very stupid actions. She really hoped Chance hadn't heard all the sordid details.

"Forget it," she said finally, tiring of whatever game he was playing to torment her. "It doesn't matter what you think you know."

"Oh, I know quite a bit," he taunted. "Wilkie was feeling talkative when I got home last night."

"Really?" Jenny said, fighting to keep her tone neutral.

"Yep. He told me about how you and your mama came here all worked up about righting old injustices to your Native American ancestors. He said you'd even told Harlan that his land had really belonged to your granddaddy and that, by rights, it should be yours." He regarded her speculatively. "Was he telling the truth about all that?"

"I suppose," she muttered, seeing now why he'd drawn the comparison between the two of them.

Chance grinned. "Thought so. Wilkie's not prone to telling tall tales. So how did you and Harlan work it out? The way I have it figured, your mama took the easy way of assuring she got what she wanted. She married Harlan to make sure she got your ancestors' land back, right?"

"Of all the twisted, outrageous accusations," Jenny sputtered. "How could you even think such a thing without ever having met her or having seen the two of them together? She married him because she loves him. She's not getting one acre of his land."

"And you? What's your stake in White Pines?"

She hesitated for a moment, then admitted, "I'm entitled to the same share as Luke, Cody, Jordan and Lizzy—one-fifth of the land. I never even asked for that, by the way. It was Harlan's idea. He drew up the papers and gave them to my mom on their wedding day. Cody's the one who actually gets the ranching operation, though. We've all agreed he's entitled to it after all the work he's done over the years. His son, Harlan Patrick, will probably take it over after him, if he can stop chasing girls long enough to concentrate on learning the business side of things."

"I see."

Something in his tone alerted Jenny that she'd just blabbed an important piece of family business. Not that the division of White Pines was much of a secret. Everybody in town had probably guessed the terms of Harlan's will, including the chatty Wilkie. Some were purely speculating. Others had probably wrangled insider information from one Adams or another. They all knew exactly how Harlan's estate had been set up. He thought each of them had a right to know where they stood so there would be no wrangling among themselves after he was gone.

That didn't mean she had to confirm all the details for this man who was so intent on disrupting everyone's lives. That was her problem—she was impulsive. She tended to open her mouth and say whatever was on her mind without thinking about the consequences. Add the fact that Chance could probably charm a spiteful old spinster out of her life's savings, and she was bound to blab way too much sooner or later.

"I have to be going," she said, backing away. She didn't like the fact that she had a hard time doing it. It was as if there were an invisible force pulling them toward each other. She actually had to consciously fight to escape it.

"Scared of getting caught with me again?" he asked, amusement twinkling in his eyes as he glanced toward the drugstore.

"I'm not scared of much," she retorted.

Despite her claim, she followed his gaze toward

the window just the same to be sure that Dani and Sharon Lynn weren't peering out. If they were, Jenny would never hear the end of it. They might not be able to make out the words being exchanged, but Chance's presence alone would be enough to stir them up, especially Dani.

Assured that the two women were still at the soda fountain, she added, "Most folks around here know I'm a risk taker."

"Really?" His tone was filled with disbelief. He trailed a finger down her cheek, his eyes fastened on hers. "What kind of risks are you in the habit of taking, Jenny?"

She felt the heat climbing into her face. A quick little shiver danced down her spine. She prayed Chance wasn't aware of either, but the quirk of his lips suggested otherwise. He knew he affected her. He knew he scared her more than the prospect of tripping over a rattler in the desert.

"Have dinner with me again," he suggested softly, still caressing her cheek. "Just the two of us. Two grown-ups with an attraction that needs exploring."

"I don't think so," Jenny said, exasperated at being barely able to get the words past the yearning clogging her throat.

"Must be scared, after all," Chance said.

"I am not scared," Jenny insisted. "It just doesn't make sense for you and me to spend a whole lot of time together. It's asking for trouble."

"Why? Because you're afraid you'll stop fighting me one of these days and we'll wind up in bed?"

"Absolutely not," she replied at once, probably with a little too much vehemence. "Why would I be afraid of something that I would never in a million years allow to happen?"

Chance grinned. "A simple no would have been sufficient."

"I doubt it," she said defensively. "The word doesn't seem to register with you. Maybe you haven't heard it enough."

"I understand the concept," he said dryly. "I can also tell the difference between conviction and desperation. You, sweet thing, sounded just a trifle desperate."

Jenny stared at him in disbelief. "What on earth would I have to be desperate about?"

"Oh, I think you're downright panicky that you won't be able to persuade me to back off, and that one of these days you'll just give in to what you're feeling."

"That is absolutely ridiculous," she declared, despite the fact that he was right on the money. She didn't like the wickedly sensual feelings that came over her when he so much as grazed her cheek with his finger, much less the heart-stopping breathlessness stirred up by his kiss. She couldn't control them and she really liked being in control of herself and her destiny. Always had, ever since she'd been uprooted from New York all those years ago without any say in the matter.

"We'll see," he said, his voice low and husky.

"We will not see. I am not changing my mind."

"I'll give you a few days to think it over," he said, clearly pleased with himself for the magnanimous gesture.

Exasperated, Jenny poked a finger into the middle of his chest. "Save your breath. Ask anyone around town just how stubborn an Adams can be."

He laughed at that. "Darlin', that's just the point. You might have the name. You might have latched on to the habit of being contrary. But I'm the one with Adams blood running through my veins. When it comes to stubborn, I'd say you've met your match."

He was still chuckling when Jenny whirled away and took off as if a herd of cattle was stampeding down the road behind her.

Jenny broke every speed limit between Los Piños and the gates at White Pines, cussing a blue streak the entire way. Chance Adams figured at the center of that blue streak. Low-down sneaky scoundrel was one of the milder labels she pinned on him.

The truth was, he had shaken her. In fact, she couldn't recall the last time any man had shaken her so badly. She had stood on the sidewalk in front of Dolan's caught in the grip of emotions so powerful and so conflicting it had taken her the entire trip home to sort them out.

More than once she had wanted to slug the man, to land a shot to that handsome square jaw that would prove to him once and for all she was not a woman to be messed with.

Then, an equal number of times, she had felt very much like throwing herself into his arms and kissing him again. Only the nearby presence of Dani and Sharon Lynn, not good judgment, had kept her from acting on the almost irresistible desire to discover if his kisses were consistently bone melting, or if the one she'd experienced had been a once-in-a-lifetime aberration.

How was it possible for a man to stir such contradictory reactions, especially in the space of a few heartbeats? How was it possible she could feel anything but contempt for a man who threatened the happiness of her family? Was she simply edging toward middle-aged desperation, after all? Was she subconsciously feeling the ticking of her biological clock? Or was it specifically Chance who had the ability to turn her inside out?

Not that for one single instant the thought of marriage had entered her head, she told herself staunchly. Chance didn't make her think about marriage or babies or growing old together. He made her think about sex. Big difference. *Huge* difference. She sighed. Intolerable difference.

She bounded up the front steps and stormed through the front door, slamming it behind her with enough force to rattle it on its hinges.

Naturally, because he was the last person she wanted to see, her father was standing at the foot of the stairs, staring at her with a thoroughly bemused expression.

"Bad day?" he inquired lightly.

"You could say that."

"Want to talk about it?"

"Not especially," she said, then recalled her vow to fill her father in on the dinner she'd had with Chance. Now she had today's encounter to add to the confession. She forced a rueful smile. "I take it back. Do you feel like going for a walk?"

"Sure."

Jenny turned around and headed back outside, taming her pace to suit her father's slower gait.

"Where to?" he asked when they reached the bottom of the front steps.

Jenny shrugged. "Doesn't matter."

"Then let's head out to the stables. I want to take a look at the new broodmare Cody paid an arm and a leg for."

She slanted an amused look at him. "Cody's throwing your money around again?"

Her father chuckled. "There's nothing he enjoys more. Not that he's made a bad investment yet," he conceded. "Just don't tell him I said that."

"Don't you think maybe it's time to let him know you approve of the way he runs things around here?"

Her father gave her a startled look. "You think he doesn't know?"

"I think it wouldn't hurt to remind him every

once in a while just in case he takes your constant grumbling to heart.''

Harlan nodded slowly. "You could have a point," he conceded. "Now why don't you tell me what's on your mind? Who's been picking on you? Do I need to get out my shotgun and wave it around?''

She looked at his fierce expression and smiled. "You would, too, wouldn't you?''

"If somebody hurt one of my kids or my grand-babies, you bet I would.''

Impulsively Jenny stopped and hugged him, then planted a kiss on his weathered cheek. "Thank you.''

He seemed startled by the gesture, but clearly it pleased him. "What was that for?''

"For treating me like one of your kids.''

"Great heavenly days, you *are* one of my kids, Jenny, my girl. I've never thought of you any other way.''

His emphatic response warmed her heart, but it also deepened her fear she was the worst sort of traitor. "How would you feel if one of your kids betrayed you?'' she asked, her tone barely above a whisper.

This time he was the one who halted. He searched her face intently. "You think that's what you've done?''

"Some people in the family think I have.''

"That's not the same as you believing it, is it?''

"No.''

"Why don't you just tell me what happened and let me decide for myself?"

She forced a smile. "Easier said than done. I'm scared you'll agree with them."

"And do what? Hate you? Disown you? It won't happen, Jenny, my girl. You're family. We'll work it out. You being straight with me now will go a long way toward fixing things, assuming they even need repair in the first place."

Reassured by that promise, she described her dinner with Chance and all the events that had led up to it. "Then today, not two seconds after leaving Dani and Sharon Lynn, I ran smack into him again and there we were, in plain view of everyone, talking."

"Talking, huh? On a public sidewalk? To a man who happened along?" Her father's eyes twinkled with amusement. "Now that is cause for concern. I declare, I've never heard such goings-on."

"You're making fun of me," she accused. "I'm serious."

"I can see that," he said, his expression turning more somber. "But, darlin' girl, I am not going to lose any sleep because you spent a little time with Chance Adams. The truth is, I'd like to meet the man myself."

Stunned, she stared at him. "You would?"

"Don't look so shocked. Of course I would. I might not agree with what he intends to do, but he's my brother's son. And that son of his, Petey, sounds like Luke and Cody when they were boys. Seems to me they'd both probably fit right in with the rest of us if we gave them the opportunity. Chance is the one who wants to turn White Pines into a battle-ground and me into the enemy. It's not the other way around.''

"But no matter which one starts it, isn't it all the same in the end?" Jenny asked. "If he's determined to claim what he thinks is his, then we *are* pitted against each other, like it or not."

"I suppose that depends on what you and the others determine is the right thing to do under the circumstances. I gave all of you the choice of how to handle this.''

"Well, obviously Dani, at least, is gearing up for a fight. She must be getting that from Jordan.''

He seemed surprised by her uncertainty over the views of the rest of the family. "Haven't you talked to any of the others?''

"Not since they were here for dinner.''

"Maybe it's time you all sat down and thrashed it out. We could get this settled once and for all.''

"Maybe so,'' she agreed with a sigh.

He regarded her intently. "Let me ask you something. Aside from this battle over White Pines, what do you think of Chance?''

She thought about the question, determined to answer it as honestly as she could. "He seems like a decent man. He's a good father and, from what I gather, he's a loyal son. He's also arrogant and handsome and stubborn.''

Her father chuckled. "Sound like anyone else you've ever met?"

"Every Adams man on earth," she conceded.

"Then he can't be all bad, can he?" Harlan pressed his callused palm to her cheek and gazed directly into her eyes. "Darlin' girl, you make up your own mind about Chance Adams, and you decide what sort of relationship you want to have with him. Trust your own judgment."

"I can't bear the thought of everyone in the family thinking I'm betraying you. You're the most important person in the world to me, besides mom."

"Well, when it comes to that, I'm the only one you have to worry about," he reminded her. "And I've just told you where I stand. If anyone else wants to make a fuss, send 'em to me. I'll set 'em straight."

"Somehow I don't think even you will be able to appease Dani and the others."

"Then you do want to spend more time with the man?"

"Yes," she said impulsively, then promptly retracted it. "I mean no. It's just…I'm sure we're going to be thrown together from time to time because of Petey."

"Is that all you're worried about?"

"Yes," she insisted.

"Okay, then. You're a teacher. It's your job to deal with the parents of your students. You can't treat Chance Adams any differently than you would any other parent in town. If anybody in the family questions you, just tell them that. Then tell 'em to go to blazes."

Jenny grinned. "Who'll pick me up off the ground when they punch my lights out?"

"I will."

"Thank you," she said, hugging him again.

Her father wrapped his arms around her and held her tightly. Then he stood back and gazed warmly into her eyes. "If you should change your mind and decide that your interest in this man is personal, that would be okay, too," he said quietly.

When Jenny would have moved away to argue, he held her in place. "Just listen to me for once," he commanded. "Real love's a scarce commodity in this life. When it comes along, only a fool turns his back on it."

"I never said anything about love," Jenny protested. She wasn't in love with Chance. She still wasn't sure if she even liked him very much.

Her father chuckled. "You didn't have to."

This time she did pull away. "Don't you dare go getting any ideas about me and Chance Adams," she ordered, realizing exactly where his thoughts were headed. "I am not going to become one of your little matchmaking projects."

"Of course not," he said agreeably. "You're a grown woman. You can pick and choose your own friends, settle on your own husband. I'm just saying, if you were to settle on Chance, it would be okay."

"Oh, for goodness' sake," she began, then decided to save the protest. He clearly wouldn't believe anything she had to say about Chance meaning absolutely nothing to her. Once Harlan Adams's romantic fantasies stirred to life, no one was more dedicated to the promotion of a good love story. Anything she said would only encourage him.

"I'm going back to the house," she said.

"I'll say it again, darlin' girl. Don't turn your back on your heart. Listen to what it has to say."

"I know exactly what my heart is saying," she retorted. "And it is not saying anything about Chance Adams."

"Maybe it's just not saying anything you want to hear."

"Pardon me for saying this, Daddy, but go to blazes."

He stared at her for an instant, then threw back his head and laughed. "Whoo-ee! It's about to get real interesting around here."

As she walked away, Jenny realized it was the second time that day she had provided a man with so much entertainment. Adams men! Darned if they weren't all alike.

Chapter Seven

Wilkie Rollins's books were a disgrace. Chance had spent every evening for the past two months trying to untangle the mess the old man had made of his ranch finances. Wilkie claimed the details didn't matter to him, as long as he had money in the bank at the end of the month.

The disorder made Chance edgy. He'd insisted on setting them right so Wilkie would know how Chance's management of the place was going.

"Son, I can see the kind of job you're doing by looking around," Wilkie had countered. "I don't need to see the books to get an answer."

Chance had been appalled. "Wilkie, you can't run a ranch like that. How will you ever know if you're being cheated?"

His boss had looked him up and down. "You intend on cheating me?"

Chance had waved off the ridiculous question. "No, of course not. If I'd intended to, I never would have brought up the books in the first place."

"Well, then, I don't see that we've got a problem."

Chance had given up after that. He was still intent on straightening out the bookkeeping, but he was doing it more for his own satisfaction than for Wilkie's. Besides, he liked making order out of chaos. He'd been doing that most of his life. Hank hadn't exactly been a paragon of orderliness, and Chance's mother had been more eager to please Hank than keep the household running smoothly.

From the time he could reach the stove, Chance had done most of the cooking, albeit even then it had been limited mostly to frozen dinners and fresh vegetables. He'd also done a good bit of the cleaning, in addition to whatever chores Hank had allotted him. It had given him a sense of structure that hadn't been forthcoming from his parents. He'd always prided himself on seeing that Petey had rules and routine, even if Hank had taken equal pride in seeing that his grandson broke most of them.

Chance was trying to make sense of a column of receipts when he realized Petey was standing beside him. He glanced up from the accounting ledger into solemn blue eyes.

"Hey, what's up?"

"You busy?" Petey asked.

"It's nothing that can't wait. You got something on your mind?"

"Sort of."

"What?"

"It's school."

One simple word—school—and Chance's blood surged as if he'd been shown an album of erotica. Images of Miss Prim and Prissy looking all mussed and kissable lit up in his mind like neon.

"Did something happen today?" he asked when he thought he could get the words out without sounding ridiculously breathless.

"Something happened all right. That lady punished me!" Petey blurted, his little body radiating indignation. "I thought she was supposed to be your friend. I told you she wasn't. I told you she was that bad man's daughter and that made her bad, too, but you didn't believe me."

Chance sighed. He should have known one dinner would not build a bridge between those two, not with Petey so determinedly loyal to his grandfather. He couldn't help wondering why he'd heard none of this from Jenny herself this afternoon. Had her silence on the topic been deliberate or had she simply been distracted by her session with Dani and Sharon Lynn? Maybe she'd just been rattled by his presence. That possibility brought him a very large measure of satisfaction.

"Dad," Petey complained, "you're not paying attention."

"Okay. Sorry. Why don't you tell me exactly

what happened?'' he suggested, keeping his tone neutral.

''She yelled at me in front of the whole class,'' Petey began, then drew a deep breath as he gathered momentum. ''And then she made me go into the hall and told me I was going to grow up and be ignorant.''

Chance bristled on his son's behalf, but reason told him Petey was only relaying part of the story. ''Why did she yell at you in the first place?''

Petey stared down at the floor. ''I don't know.''

''Excuse me?'' Chance said. ''You have absolutely no idea why your teacher was yelling at you? Was it just out of the blue? Did she jump up and pick you out of a whole roomful of kids to humiliate?''

''What's humiliate?''

''Never mind. The point is, I can't help thinking that Ms. Adams must have had a good reason for yelling. I'm also thinking I'd rather hear that reason from you. You might prefer that as well, because if I get an explanation from her, it will probably irritate the dickens out of me and I might be inclined to yell at you, too.''

Petey stared back at him with a wide innocent look. Tears pooled in the corners of his eyes. Chance felt like a louse, but he refused to back down. He was beginning to get an idea of just what Jenny was up against. He wasn't quite ready to be sympathetic, but a few more incidents and he might be forced to shift his allegiance.

"I'm waiting," he said quietly.

"It wasn't anything really bad," Petey said finally. "It wasn't like I chopped off a girl's braid or something."

"I'm relieved. What was it, then?"

"I put some glue down," he mumbled.

Chance had a sinking sensation in the pit of his stomach. Glue and Petey were a dangerous combination. He could tell already that he wasn't going to like the rest of the story. "Where?"

"On some papers."

"What papers?"

"The math test papers."

Chance stared at his son in stunned disbelief. "You glued the math test papers together? Is that what you're telling me?" he demanded, his voice climbing.

"It's not like she couldn't make more copies," Petey said defensively.

"Then this was a test you hadn't taken yet, correct?"

"Yeah, I mean, it was just a joke. You can see that, can't you?" Petey asked, his tone pleading. "She can always give the test tomorrow when she has more copies, right?"

Chance was tempted to send Petey straight to his room and ground him until he reached puberty, but he figured there were a couple of additional things he needed to know first.

"Why did you do this?"

"What do you mean, why?"

"I mean what the dickens were you thinking?" Chance shouted.

Petey's expression faltered. "Now you're yelling at me, too."

"For good reason," Chance said, but he managed to lower his voice. "Did you glue these papers together, by any chance, because you hadn't studied for the test?"

"Not exactly. Besides, math's my best subject. You know that. I could have passed it, anyway."

"Then why?" An idea began taking shape, an idea that made all too much sense. "Wait, let me guess. Timmy McPherson hadn't studied for the math test, had he?"

"Jeez, Dad, you know I can't tell you that," Petey exclaimed. "That would be, like, tattling."

"Okay, we'll let that pass," Chance said, concluding it would be a waste of time to deliver another lecture on the folly of protecting a kid who appeared to be dedicated to destroying Petey's life. "I think I know the answer. Besides, the important thing here is that you did something you knew was wrong. Again," he added. "What was Ms. Adams's punishment?"

"I told you, she made me go into the hall and she told me I was gonna grow up ignorant."

"I'd say she let you off lightly." Chance looked directly into his son's eyes, then added pointedly, "Way more lightly than I intend to let you off."

Petey stared back at him in horror. "You're gonna punish me, too?"

"Oh, yeah," Chance said grimly. "You will get off the school bus every afternoon for the next week and go directly to your room. You will double your homework assignments. If Ms. Adams gives you five math problems, you'll do ten. If she assigns ten pages in your history book, you will read twenty. I want her to send me a written list of your assignments so I can sign off that you've done the work. Got it?"

"No way," Petey said, clearly shaken. "I'll be up all night."

"Missing a little sleep won't hurt you. Besides, you'll have all weekend to get ahead."

"What are you saying? I can't even go outside this weekend?"

"You've got it, pal."

Petey shot him a rebellious look. "Who's gonna make me stay in my room?"

"I will. If I'm not here, I'll hire a baby-sitter."

Petey looked doubly horrified. "A baby-sitter? You can't. I'm too old. I'll never be able to show my face in school again if anyone finds out you've hired some girl to baby-sit me."

"Then I guess you'll think long and hard before you misbehave in school again, won't you?"

"But, Dad—"

Chance shook his head. "No buts, pal. You brought this one on yourself."

"It's not fair!" Petey protested. "You're siding with the enemy!"

"Ms. Adams is not the enemy, not in the classroom. She's in charge there. We've been over this before.''

"But—''

"There's no point in arguing. Go to your room now. I'm sure you have a lot of homework left to do.''

"I hate you!'' Petey yelled as he raced from the room. "And Granddad would hate you, too, if he knew you were picking her over your own kid!''

Maybe so, Chance conceded to himself when Petey was gone. But Hank wasn't the one trying to get a kid through school without winding up in juvenile court.

He had to bear some of the responsibility for this. He obviously hadn't made his displeasure over the hair-chopping incident plain enough to his son. Even after their dinner together Petey clearly thought making Jenny Adams's life a living hell was within bounds.

Well, it had to stop. No one was going to find some way to say he wasn't a fit parent. He'd get Petey under control.

Besides, if anybody in this family was going to keep Jenny all riled up, it was going to be him. He was already enjoying it way more than he ought to.

Chance wasn't certain exactly what drew him to White Pines on Saturday. He was still feeling guilty about Petey's misbehavior, and maybe on some level he wanted to make amends. Or it might have been the simple desire to catch his first up-close look at the ranch his father had been obsessed with most of his life. Maybe he'd just run out of the willpower he needed to stay away.

More than likely, though, it had something to do with his need to butt heads with Jenny. Clashing with her just on general principle made him feel more alive than he'd imagined possible a few short months ago when he'd been grieving the loss of Mary and his father.

With Petey settled in for the day and the dreaded teenage baby-sitter keeping guard, Chance took the highway in front of Wilkie's and headed west in the direction of the family ranch. He'd traveled the same road at least a dozen times since arriving in town a few months back, but he'd always stopped well short of the gate to White Pines. He'd vowed he wouldn't set foot on the land until it belonged to him.

Today, however, he broke that vow. He turned in and drove slowly down the long winding lane, absorbing his first impression of the land around him. It was ruggedly beautiful, as he'd known it would be. His father had described it endlessly, his voice thick with emotion. And Wilkie's neighboring property gave a hint of what he could expect. It was just that White Pines had more of it. Acres and acres more. The endless view was awesome.

Chance's first sight of the house, though, had him hitting the brakes and wondering if he'd taken a wrong turn. Apparently his father's memory had failed him here, or else Harlan Adams had spent a small fortune restoring the place to its original glory.

Chance cut the truck's engine eventually, but he couldn't stop staring. There was a strong hint of the old South to the house. That much his father had recalled. But in his stories, the house had been virtually tumbling down, a mere shadow of the dream home his ancestors had built when they'd come west after the Civil War. Hank had talked of grand rooms from which the furnishings had been sold off piece by piece to pay the bills. He had described ragged drapes and scarred paint.

The house certainly wasn't suffering from such inattention now. Freshly painted a pristine white, its pillars impressive, if out of place in West Texas, its gardens a riot of color, the mansion could have been transported back to the South and not suffered by comparison to its neighbors.

The sweep of the porch—he supposed it ought to be called a veranda or some such—was such a far cry from the tiny two-rocker porch on Hank's cabin back in Montana that it left Chance awestruck. He wondered if the family sat out here at sunset, watching the changing colors on the horizon, or if they just took the wonder of it all for granted.

There had to be twenty rooms inside, he thought as he continued to sit and stare, trying to absorb the grandeur of it. More, probably. For just an instant he wondered what the devil he'd do with twenty rooms—or even ten, if they split the place down the middle. Then he banished the thought as irrelevant.

Half of White Pines—house and land—was his. That was all that mattered. He could close off every room but one if he wanted to. The point was, it would be his choice to make.

Pushing aside an unexpected surge of uncertainty, he climbed out of his pickup, settled his hat on his head and strode up the front steps, steeled for the bitter confrontation that was bound to come, especially if anyone other than Jenny answered the door.

He hadn't exactly considered what he was going to say to whichever stranger answered his forceful knock on that heavy, carved front door. The sound of footsteps slowed his pulse to a dull thud. Maybe he was making a terrible mistake by coming. He should have thought this moment through, planned more carefully for it.

It was too late now, though. The door swung wide and he was suddenly face-to-face with a silver-haired, stoop-shouldered, yet still impressive man who had to be Harlan Adams. The family resemblance between him and Hank was stunning. In recent years Hank had been thinner, but both men had the same clear blue eyes, the same square jaw.

Chance stared at Harlan Adams, suddenly feeling oddly tongue-tied. He told himself it was fury that silenced him, but it was more. Much more. It was history and family and pride, all kicking in with a swell of contradictory emotions.

His uncle, however, had no such reticence. "You must be Chance," he said quietly, his gaze even and unblinking. If he was thrown by the surprise arrival of his nephew, he hid it well. He held out his hand, closed it in a firm grip around Chance's. "I'm Harlan Adams, your uncle."

"I'm surprised you recognize me," Chance said stiffly, returning the handshake he'd been too startled to ignore.

The comment drew a broad smile. "Come on in," Harlan said with what appeared to be unforced graciousness. "I'll show you why."

Chance followed his uncle into a living room that was three times as big as his own and filled with comfortable furniture that was obviously expensive but surprisingly unpretentious. Harlan followed his gaze and said, "The place used to be filled with antiques, but Jenny got tired of tippytoeing around in here. Next thing I knew, her mama had redecorated. This suits us. It's a room you can live in without being scared of breaking something every time you move. When Jenny was a teenager, that was especially important. She tended to be rambunctious."

"I can imagine," Chance said wryly, wishing for just an instant that he had known her then, that their relationship could have started off in some uncomplicated way. He suspected she would have made his heart pound and his mouth go dry even then.

Harlan led the way to a piano sitting in front of a huge bay window. Sunlight spilled through the window and glinted off the glass on literally dozens of formal photographs and snapshots. For Chance, looking at some of those pictures was like looking in a mirror.

But the absence of one picture in particular stuck in his craw. There was no snapshot of Hank Adams, no formal portrait of his grandparents with Hank and Harlan. It was as if his father had never existed, as if he'd been cut out of the universe as easily as he'd been cut out of the will.

Harlan took first one picture in hand, then another, explaining who was in each, proudly showing off his family, right down through the grandchildren, most of whom were now too darned grown-up to suit him, he claimed.

"I'm starting with great-grandbabies now, though," he said, showing off another half-dozen snapshots of a squalling newborn and a couple of boys who looked like twins and didn't look at all like Adamses.

"These two belong to Duke Jenkins," Harlan said, apparently seeing Chance's confusion. "He just married my granddaughter Dani, so, of course, now they're family, too. Born, adopted, it doesn't matter. They're all family."

The pride, the love shining in his eyes, all of it was too much for Chance. He wanted to smash every single one of those pictures. Harlan Adams thought more of these great-grandchildren who hadn't even been born to an Adams than he did of his own brother.

Instead of saying that, though, instead of railing against the injustice of it, Chance kept his cool and solidified his determination. This little exhibition had fueled his determination for battle just when he might have been tempted by his fascination with Jenny into tempering it. That didn't mean he would leave here today without catching a glimpse of her.

"Is Jenny around?" he asked eventually.

Harlan regarded him speculatively. "Is that why you really came? To see Jenny?"

Chance nodded. "I need to talk to her about my boy. He's been giving her a rough time in school."

"So I've heard," Harlan said, chuckling. "I'd like to meet him. He sounds like my sons way back when. They were up to mischief all the time."

"That's Petey, all right."

"Why don't you bring him along next time you come?"

Surprised by the invitation, Chance nodded. "Maybe I will—if there is a next time."

"Why wouldn't there be?"

"I just thought..." Chance shrugged. "Never mind. You never did say if Jenny was around."

"She's gone for a ride with her sister," Harlan said. "They should be back soon. Or if you'd like, we could saddle up and go out and find them. It would give you a chance to look the place over."

Even more startled by this invitation, Chance had to wonder if Harlan realized what he was offering. He was giving the enemy a chance to size up the potential spoils of this family war. His uncle's bland expression, however, gave nothing away.

"I'm surprised," Chance confessed.

"By?"

"The fact that you didn't kick me off the property. Most men would have."

His uncle seemed genuinely puzzled by the suggestion. "Why would I do that?" he asked, then added simply, "You're my brother's boy."

"A brother you ran off," Chance retorted bitterly.

"Something I will regret to my dying day," Harlan said with apparent sincerity. "I was sorry to hear he'd passed away. I wish we'd had a chance for me to make amends. Someday, if you like, we can talk about that."

"I don't need to talk about it. I know the details."

"From your father's perspective," his uncle said. "There are two sides to every story. A wise man listens to both before making up his mind. Whether you do or not, though, you'll always be welcome here."

Chance stared at him in amazement. "Even though I intend to do everything in my power to take it away from you?" he asked.

Harlan actually had the audacity to smile at that. "Give it your best shot, son. Nothing gets the blood to flowing like a good brawl."

Chance's respect for the man deepened in that instant. Under other conditions he had a feeling he could actually like Harlan Adams.

But there were no other conditions. History stood between them, just as it did between him and Jenny. Not that it was stopping him where she was concerned, he thought ruefully.

"I think I'd like to ride out with you," he said.

Harlan gave a brisk nod of satisfaction. "Good. I'll get my coat. There's a chill in the air today, and these old bones of mine don't take to the cold they way they once did."

"Maybe you'd rather just point the way."

"No, indeed. I go for a ride every day just to see the beauty of this land. I've got the time to appreciate it now, and I never let a day pass without letting the good Lord know I'm grateful." His expression turned wistful. "Can't go quite as far as I once could, though. Hopefully we'll come across Jenny and Lizzy before I tire out, and then Jenny can show you what I can't."

"Thank you," Chance felt compelled to say, though it grated at him to thank this man for anything. "You've been very kind."

Harlan squeezed his shoulder. "No reason not to be." His gaze narrowed. "One word of warning, though. I'll fight you fair and square over White Pines, but you do one single thing to hurt Jenny and you'll live to regret it."

Chance nodded, not surprised at all that Harlan Adams had intuitively sensed that his interest in Jenny was dangerous. "Fair enough."

The line had been drawn in the sand, so to speak. It suited Chance's need for order. It also told him that Harlan Adams was a man with clear priorities. He might love his land, he might even fight for it if forced to, but his children were his life. In that instant Chance wondered for the first time how a man who felt that strongly about family could have turned his back on his younger brother.

Maybe, just maybe, his father hadn't told him the whole story, after all.

Chapter Eight

In the midst of spreading a blanket on the ground for the picnic she and Lizzy had brought with them on their ride, Jenny thought she heard the sound of hooves. She glanced toward the southeast and spotted two men on horseback heading their way at a leisurely pace. She recognized her father at once, but the man beside him almost looked like Chance, which, of course, was impossible. He would never show up at White Pines. Nor was her father likely to welcome him, except maybe with a shotgun blast or dueling pistols.

Then again, he had said just a few nights ago that he wanted to meet his brother's son.

"Lizzy, can you see who's riding with Daddy?" Jenny asked.

Her younger sister looked up from the picnic basket Maritza had packed and stared in the direction Jenny indicated. "I've never seen him before, which is too bad, because he is one hundred percent gorgeous," Lizzy declared breathlessly. She automatically reached up to tidy her naturally curly black hair, which she'd scooped into a careless ponytail.

Jenny fought back amusement. Lizzy was at the age when her fascination with men was increasing by the same leaps and bounds as her hormones. Jenny couldn't recall ever being quite so over-the-top about the opposite sex in general and only once about a specific man. The latter had occurred all too recently. She was still trying very hard to pretend that it was nothing more than a wild fantasy taking control of her body.

Lizzy's brow wrinkled as she peered more intently at the riders. "He looks a little like Cody, don't you think, only younger?"

Jenny sighed heavily at the description. It was Chance. It had to be. He was the only man she knew who might be mistaken for Cody. Not even Cody's own son resembled him as closely. Harlan Patrick was still gangly, while Cody, like Chance, was solid muscle.

Lizzy stared at her worriedly. "What's wrong? Do you know who it is?"

"Possibly."

"Who?"

"My hunch is you're about to meet Chance Adams."

Her sister's eyes widened. "Our long-lost cousin? The man who wants White Pines?"

"The one and only."

"Oh, dear. What do you suppose he's doing with Daddy?"

"Scoping out the property, I imagine," Jenny said wryly.

"Daddy looks okay from here. You don't suppose they fought or something, do you? Maybe Chance kidnapped him and forced him to take him on a tour."

Jenny had briefly considered the very same scenario, but it was ridiculous of course. Chance was perfectly civilized, if misguided in his intentions. Besides, from this distance, both men looked un-bloodied, which must mean this first meeting had gone passably well. She would have expected as much of her father. He was an amazingly tolerant man and he'd flat out told her he was anxious to meet his nephew.

Chance, though, was another story. He was just itching for a fight. From the moment he'd explained what he was doing in Los Piños, it had been clear he wouldn't be happy until he'd paid his uncle back for the sins he believed had been committed against his father.

So what was he doing here today? Jenny wondered. Was it as simple as taking a look around? Or was he setting his plan into motion finally? And why was his gaze fixed so avidly on her as they neared? The intensity of it could have set off a forest fire from a hundred yards back. It certainly set off a lickety-split pace of her pulse.

Before Jenny could reach any conclusions about what his presence might mean, Lizzy gave an exuberant shout and raced off to meet their father. At least she was still one part little girl, Jenny thought, watching her race across the open field. Because looking at Chance unsettled her, she kept her gaze fixed on Lizzy.

Harlan bent low and gave Lizzy a hand up onto his horse, settling her on the saddle in front of him. Jenny had seen her father do the same thing a hundred times over the years, but she never failed to feel a trace of envy as she watched their rapport. Harlan might love her, might love all of them deeply, but even at twenty, Lizzy was his precious baby.

"Don't look now, but jealousy is gnawing at you," Chance observed, dismounting right beside her.

Startled by his insight and by the fact that he'd managed to sneak up on her, Jenny scowled at him. "You don't know what you're talking about."

"Oh, I think I do. You got to be queen of the roost for how long? A year, maybe two, before baby sister came along and stole your daddy's heart."

"Don't be ridiculous. I was fifteen when she was born. I was thrilled to have a baby in the house. I had no cause to be jealous."

"Maybe no cause," he said, "but jealousy's a

funny thing. It gets under the skin and eats away at logic.''

Refusing to concede he might be at least partially right, Jenny slanted a defiant look at him. ''Why are you out here today, anyway? Is this another of your less-than-subtle attempts to stir up trouble?''

''Not really. I just thought it was time to pay a friendly visit.''

''Since you claimed not to be interested in coleslaw and barbecue,'' she said, reminding him of his taunt, ''shall I assume you've come to scope out the territory for the invasion you have planned?''

He grinned at that. Jenny's traitorous heart turned an unexpected flip. For a good many years now she'd thought herself immune to a man's charms. Maybe she just hadn't met one who was half this gorgeous when he smiled. She didn't need to remind herself that this particular man was also as dangerous as a dozen rattlers. His motives were as suspect as a reformed burglar's asking to see the silver.

Harlan closed in just then. ''You two mind if I take off with Lizzy and leave you to your own devices?''

Jenny shot a panicky look at her sister. ''What about the picnic? We were just getting the food out.''

''You and Chance can have it,'' Lizzy said as she dismounted from her father's horse and climbed into the saddle on her own. ''I'd rather take a ride with Daddy. I'll eat when I get back to the house.''

''That okay with you, Chance?'' her father asked.

"I promise I'm leaving you in good hands. Jenny knows every inch of this land. She can show you anything you want to see."

"Perfect," Chance said, just as Jenny prepared to utter another desperate protest.

"I really don't think—" she tried again.

Chance cut her off. "Cousin Jenny and I will spend the time getting to know each other," he said, looping an arm over her shoulder in a display of friendliness that had Lizzy smirking and their father looking a little too pleased with himself.

"I am not your cousin," she reminded Chance fiercely under her breath.

She promptly regretted the quick retort when she saw that it stirred a suspicious gleam in Harlan's eyes. That all-too-familiar glint confirmed her worst fears. The sneaky old matchmaker really was scheming to light a spark between her and Chance. What the devil was wrong with him? That would be like inviting the wolf to make himself at home in the henhouse and then sitting back with a glass of bourbon to watch the feathers fly.

Though he'd accepted the suggestion readily enough, Chance seemed to be wondering about his uncle's motivation, too. He followed Harlan's departure with a puzzled expression on his face. When he turned back to Jenny, though, the gleam in his eyes suggested he was far more fascinated with her than he was with Harlan's behavior.

Jenny recognized that gleam for exactly what it was. She might be living on a ranch in the middle of some half-baked deserted part of Texas, but she'd spent her first fourteen years on the streets of New York. She'd spent most of the past ten years lobbying in Washington, where the halls of Congress were every bit as mean as the streets of Manhattan. She wasn't naive. She wasn't anybody's fool. And she wasn't about to become some pawn in the war between Chance Adams and his uncle.

"Forget it," she said as firmly as if she were in the classroom and Chance were a mischievous student. She deliberately turned her back on him and busied herself with setting out the food Maritza had prepared. If it had been up to her, she would have packed it up again and headed straight for home, but she knew exactly how Chance would interpret that. He'd love to have more evidence that he disconcerted her.

"Forget what?" he inquired in a lazy way that was about as innocent as pure sin. He took a step closer, casting a shadow over her.

Jenny shivered. Her heart fluttered. Despite the unexpected chill that had come over her when he'd blocked out the sun, her skin heated. Her throat dried up like the desert in the middle of a drought.

"Whatever," she barely managed to choke out.

"You mean this?" he asked quietly as he hunkered down beside her and tucked a finger under her chin to tilt it up. He lowered his head without warning. His lips skimmed lightly over hers, teasing, taunting, until her knees felt weak and her resolve turned to mush. It was a good thing that she was already kneeling. That way, it didn't look quite so obvious when she sank spinelessly onto the blanket. Chance followed her down, his lips still firmly locked with hers.

The kiss was greedy and all-consuming. Pretty soon, with her resolve long since in tatters, Jenny lost herself in it. With a sense of wonder she discovered that his mouth felt like cool satin and tasted like peppermint. His cheeks were rough with just a hint of stubble, and his thick sun-streaked hair slid through her fingers like strands of silk. She breathed deeply and drank in the masculine scent of him, all musky heat and soap with just a hint of coconut. She smiled when she recognized that the last was sunscreen lotion.

"You smell like summer at the beach," she murmured without thinking.

A lazy smile broke over his face. "That must bring back good memories. You're actually smiling at me for a change."

Startled and furious with herself for yielding to temptation, she backed away until the width of the blanket was between them.

"It's not going to work," she declared staunchly when she finally managed to drag some air back into her lungs.

"Sure it is, darlin'," he declared with absolute confidence in his powers of persuasion.

"A kiss doesn't mean anything," she insisted.

"Maybe not one, but sometimes they start to add

up." He was still grinning. "That's when things begin to get interesting."

The comment scared her to death. She could understand exactly how that could happen. She was already growing addicted to the feel of Chance's mouth on hers. A giddy sort of anticipation rushed through her now every time she saw him. There wasn't a doubt in her mind that it could whirl out of control in no time at all.

That meant restraint was critical, she realized, her thoughts scrambling frantically in search of a plan. No more accidental encounters, though she had no idea how to go about preventing them. No more shared meals, especially not just the two of them. And absolutely positively no more kisses. That was essential.

Of course here she was, unexpectedly alone with him, an entire meal spread out on a blanket no less, and her mouth scant inches away from his and still warm from their last kiss. He looked as if he might be one breath away from stealing another.

"You're thinking too much. What's going on in that head of yours now?" Chance asked, reaching out and brushing a strand of hair back from her cheek.

The light caress sent a jolt of pure yearning slamming through her. "Nothing," she murmured shakily.

Chance sighed. "Darlin', you are a terrible liar. Now tell me the truth. What's got you worrying? Surely it's not being out here all alone with me."

Jenny debated attempting another lie, but in the end she couldn't see the point to it. Obviously she was no good at it. Maybe Chance was the kind of man who would appreciate straightforward honesty. Maybe he would even respect her enough to back off and leave her alone.

"Okay, here it is. You, me, this," she said, gesturing at the blanket with an all-encompassing wave. "This is a very bad idea. Nothing can come of it, but something will."

"Not unless you want it to," Chance countered, sketching a cross over the region of his heart.

"Oh, really," she said doubtfully. "I didn't want to kiss you, but I did, not just once but...how many times now?"

"Not nearly enough."

She shot an impatient look at him. "Stop it! Aren't you hearing anything I'm saying? The way we're begging for trouble, we might as well go into the middle of the street and wait for a speeding car to knock us down."

He frowned. "I'm not sure I like the analogy."

"Then pick one of your own," she retorted. "The point is, we have absolutely no business spending even five minutes alone together."

"Because we can't keep our hands off each other?"

"Exactly. Or at least that's part of it."

"Doesn't that tell you something?" he inquired reasonably.

"It tells me we are fools. We don't want the same things in life at all."

"Of course we do."

"How can you say that?"

"We both want White Pines, don't we? Can't you think of it this way? We're just two outsiders uniting to claim what ought to be ours."

So that was his game! Jenny backed away furiously at the suggestion that somehow the two of them were alike or that they had the same underhanded mission. She stood up, towering over him as he reclined on the blanket and watched her with that knowing amused gleam still in his eyes.

"I don't have to claim a damn thing," she practically shouted, figuring it was the only way to get anything through that thick head of his. "This is my land we're on. Mine and Lizzy's and Cody's and Jordan's and Luke's. The only way you'll get so much as an inch of it is by destroying the whole lot of us."

The tirade didn't seem to upset him at all. Without missing a beat he said, "I can think of an easier, more pleasant way to accomplish my goal." His gaze swept over her, lingering on her curves with an intensity she knew was meant to rattle her.

The tactic worked. Her insides were in turmoil. Jenny's gaze narrowed. "How?"

"Marry me."

If he'd declared his intention to stage a night raid with a band of thieves at his side, she couldn't have been more shocked. "Are you out of your mind?"

she demanded in a voice that shook with indignation.

He went on as if she hadn't said a word, "I'll settle for a fifth of the land, instead of half. Your fifth. You'll be protecting the interests of all the others."

"You *have* lost your mind," she said. "That's it, isn't it? You've flipped out, gone round the bend."

He shook his head. "Nope. I don't think so. In fact, I think I'm seeing things clearly for the first time in a very long time."

Jenny took a minute to grapple with his outrageous proposal. "How can you possibly think I'd marry you and turn over my share of White Pines to you?" she asked eventually.

"Simple. You love your father and this family he brought you into. Marrying me will solve all their problems. In essence I'll no longer be a threat. Everyone, especially your daddy, can rest easy again."

There was an insane kind of logic to it. Obviously he knew how much she loved her father, how desperately she wanted these last years of his life to be carefree. Yet the two of them, married? It was impossible.

"Have you actually thought about this?" she asked quietly, trying to inject a note of rationality into the conversation. "You don't even know me, much less love me. Your son hates my guts or thinks he does. I am rapidly reaching the point where I can't stand the sight of you. Besides which, it is more than likely my father would change his will and cut me out of it before the ink was dry on our wedding license.''

"That would never happen. He obviously loves you. I could see that watching and listening to the two of you just a moment ago."

"It would be a marriage made in hell," Jenny said, trying to get through to him how preposterous his idea was.

"That's what you say. I prefer to believe the evidence I discover every time you're in my arms. I think we're compatible. We'll get along."

"In bed maybe," she conceded. "But nobody spends every minute of every day in bed."

Chanced grinned. "Newlyweds do. We'll work out the rest after the honeymoon."

Jenny stared at him, waiting for the flash of humor in his eyes or the twitching of his lips to indicate he'd been teasing her. When neither happened, she whispered, "You're serious, aren't you?"

Chance hesitated, his expression thoughtful, then nodded. "It would be a solution."

"It would be a nightmare."

He reached over and folded her hand in his, then brushed a kiss across the knuckles. "Look, I'll admit the proposal was impulsive. It took me by surprise, the same as it did you. But it makes sense. Take some time to think it through. You'll agree with me. I'm certain of it."

"How long?" she asked, feeling desperate.

"Forty-eight hours. We'll go to dinner on Monday, someplace fancy so I can order the best bottle of champagne in the house. I'll bring along an engagement ring, something big and sparkly so you can show it off to the family.''

''Save your money,'' Jenny responded.

''Darlin', that is not an indication of open-mindedness,'' Chance chided.

''The family would be appalled if I came in and announced we were getting married. They'd never believe we'd fallen in love.''

''Then I guess we'll just have to figure out some way to convince them,'' he said, his expression unrelenting. ''Your father strikes me as the kind of man who believes in love at first sight. He'll buy it. The rest will accept it because it solves a problem.''

With her heart thumping unsteadily in her chest, Jenny felt as if her world was spinning wildly out of control. It was just as she'd feared. Her fate was out of her hands.

That made Chance's thoroughly relaxed demeanor all the more irritating. She needed some space. She also needed time, but he'd given her only forty-eight hours. She could have used a couple of years at least.

''I'm going home,'' she said abruptly.

''Before lunch?'' He looked surprised. ''Did something ruin your appetite?''

''You don't really want me to answer that, do you?''

''Come on, darlin'. Sit back down.'' He patted the space on the blanket right beside him. ''Nibble at a piece of chicken at least. You don't want the housekeeper getting the idea that you and I were out here all alone and occupied with something besides lunch, do you?''

"I don't give two hoots about the food. Leave it. You eat it. Whatever. I'll make something up to tell Maritza.''

"Such as?''

"I don't know,'' she said impatiently. "I'll tell her a storm blew up.''

Chance gestured at the clear blue sky. "Not a cloud in sight. Come on,'' he coaxed. "It would be a shame to waste a perfect fall day like this.''

He held out a barbecued chicken leg. "Looks delicious.'' When she didn't budge, he grabbed a package of brownies and waved it under her nose. "Chocolate. Don't tell me you can resist that. Something tells me you love the stuff.'' He unwrapped the brownies and took a bite of one. "Moist, rich. Best I've ever had, as a matter of fact. Sure you don't want one?''

Chocolate had always been her worst weakness, at least until she'd discovered Chance's kisses.

"Oh, for goodness' sake, give me one,'' she said irritably, snatching a brownie out of his hand. She sat down as far from him as she could possibly get on a blanket no bigger than a twin-size bed. Her blood raced at the inadvertently provocative image. Why had she made that comparison? Why was it when she looked at Chance all she thought about was tumbling into bed with him? She finished the brownie in half a dozen bites and reached for another one.

"Settled down yet?" he inquired when she was idly picking up the last crumbs.

Her gaze snapped up and clashed with his. "I don't know what you mean."

"Sure you do, darlin'. You've been in a dither ever since I rode up. I disconcert you."

"What do you expect? You propose to me out of the blue. I think it's perfectly normal to be a little unsettled."

"Then you do admit it?"

"Okay, fine. I admit it. So what?"

"Maybe we should change the subject for a minute, talk about something that doesn't get your drawers in a knot."

"Such as?"

"This latest incident with Petey."

Jenny grinned, despite herself. "I thought you wanted to talk about something that wouldn't irritate me."

"I was just going to say that I'm on your side with this one. He told me what happened. He's being punished for it. In fact, at this very moment, he's shut up in his room with a baby-sitter standing guard."

"Oh, boy, he must hate that." Jenny could almost imagine his indignation.

"That's putting it mildly."

"You can't keep him locked up forever," Jenny said, trying not to sound too wistful.

"I suspect just this once will be enough to make my point."

The words were barely out of his mouth when a rider appeared once again from the southeast. Jenny saw at once that it was Lizzy. She'd lost her hat along the way and her black hair was streaking out behind her.

"Chance!" she shouted as soon as she was close enough. "You've got to get home right away."

Even without an explanation, her tone was so urgent they were both on their feet before the words were out of Lizzy's mouth. Chance glanced at the food containers, clearly torn.

"Go," Jenny said. "I'll take care of this."

"What happened?" he asked, picking up his horse's reins as Lizzy finally reached them.

"Your baby-sitter called. Your son's disappeared."

"Oh, no," Jenny whispered as the color washed out of Chance's face. She dumped everything into the center of the blanket and tied it into a knot, then headed for her horse. "I'm coming with you," she said as she mounted.

"This isn't your problem," Chance retorted.

"It started in my classroom. Besides, if you and I go through with this crazy notion of marrying, then Petey will be my son, too. I need to help." She rode up beside her openmouthed sister and held out the picnic blanket. "Lizzy, can you take care of this for me?"

"Sure, but…married? Did you say the two of you are getting married?"

"It's a possibility," Jenny confirmed grimly. "Keep it to yourself, though. This is one piece of news I think I'd better spread around in my own good time."

"Are you coming?" Chance demanded impatiently, his horse dancing nervously in place. "You know the way back better than I do."

"Let's go," she said, kicking her horse into a gallop.

With the wind rushing in her face, the ride could have been exhilarating. Instead, Jenny kept feeling as if she was trying to outrun her destiny. Glancing over her shoulder into Chance's anxious face, she realized it was too late. For better or worse, it had already caught up with her.

Chapter Nine

Chance was cursing himself six ways from Sunday all the way back to Wilkie's place. He should have known Petey would pull a stunt like this. The kid was developing a mile-wide rebellious streak. Chance should have stuck around himself to enforce Petey's grounding, rather than deliberately fueling the boy's unhappiness by hiring a sitter.

Not that he was about to excuse what his son had done now. He'd never struck his kid, but he was very much tempted to tan his hide for sneaking off and scaring them half to death.

The baby-sitter must be beside herself. She was Wilkie's niece and she'd been hanging around the ranch ever since Chance had been hired to run the place. He suspected from some things Wilkie had said that Leesa had a crush on him. He knew very little about teenage girls, but he did know that, aside from worrying about Petey, Leesa would be distraught over having failed him.

He hit the accelerator and pushed the truck past seventy. A glance in his rearview mirror told him Jenny was right behind him. She'd insisted on bringing her own car in case they needed to expand their search and spread out in different directions. Chance hadn't wasted time arguing with her, even though he couldn't imagine how a boy on foot could get too far. Then, again, he'd never envisioned Petey slipping out of the house undetected in the first place.

Chance made the turn into Wilkie's driveway on two wheels, spewing dirt and gravel every which way. At his first glimpse of Leesa, he pulled to a stop in front of the main house. The girl was sobbing her heart out and muttering that it was all her fault. Wilkie was making a futile attempt to comfort her and assure her that nothing she could have done would have stopped Petey from sneaking out if he was of a mind to.

Chance was out of the truck before the engine stopped rumbling and heard most of the exchange. He suspected it had become repetitive by now. Wilkie stared at him helplessly over the girl's head.

"What happened?" Chance demanded. His sharp tone brought on more tears, plus a glare from Wilkie. Chance apologized. "I'm sorry, darlin'. Just try to fill me in, okay?"

"I...I don't know," Leesa finally said between sobs. "One minute he was there and the next—" she held up her hands "—he was gone. I thought for sure he was still in his room, but when I went up with a snack for him, he just wasn't there."

"How long had it been since you'd seen him?"

"A half hour at the most, I swear it. I was on the phone with one of my friends and he came down and asked for the snack. You'd told me he wasn't to be out of his room, so I said I'd bring it up to him. I got off the phone right away."

Which obviously meant nearly thirty minutes later, Chance guessed.

"And you didn't see him slip past you or hear anything that could have been him climbing out the window in his room?"

Leesa shook her head. "No. And the window wasn't open. I checked."

"Well, how the hell—" Chance stopped when Jenny shot him a warning glance.

Chance waited impatiently as Jenny took the girl in her arms and soothed her, while Wilkie looked on uncomfortably. Obviously he was no more at ease around a crying woman than Chance was. Leesa's sobs finally began to abate. Jenny glanced at him over her head and nodded.

"You searched the house?" Chance asked, forcing himself to remain calm.

"High and low," Wilkie said, appearing relieved that they'd finally gotten to a question he could answer. "The minute Leesa called me I went right over. Thought maybe the boy was playing some sort of game with her. You know how kids his age do. I've gone through every building on the property since I put out that call to you, but there's not a trace of him."

Wilkie's worried expression suggested there was more. "What else?" Chance asked.

"I think he took Golden Boy," the old man said. "The horse is missing from his stall, and no one recalls seeing him in the pasture, either."

"Well, isn't that just dandy!" Chance exploded. When Leesa burst into a fresh bout of tears, he reined in his temper. "Sorry, darlin', none of this is your fault. It's mine. I shouldn't have gone off today. I knew he resented being left with a baby-sitter and I did it, anyway, to make a point. I guess he's making one, too."

He drew a deep breath and tried to think. If Petey was on horseback, where would he head? He didn't know Los Piños all that well yet. How far could he venture before he became lost and confused?

"Chance?"

Jenny's soft voice snapped him back to reality. "What? Do you have an idea?" he asked.

"Does he know the way to White Pines?"

"Of course he does," he said as the obvious answer dawned on him. "And you're right. That's more than likely exactly where he'd head, because I've forbidden him to go over there."

"Then it's even more likely he'd go if he knew that's where you'd intended to go today," she suggested. "He wouldn't want to miss the opportunity to see the ranch he'd heard so much about from his grandfather."

Chance wasn't sure if Petey had guessed his destination or not. He hadn't told him. In fact, if Petey had figured it out, then he might go anywhere except the family ranch. Chance preferred to count on the likelihood that Petey was intent on defying him. In that case, the forbidden White Pines would be the first place he'd go.

"He wasn't on the road," Chance said thoughtfully. "We'd have spotted him."

"Maybe I can help with that. He's been asking about where the White Pines property butts up against this ranch," Wilkie explained. "He seemed to know they connected somewhere. I didn't think much about it at the time, but I'll bet he was storing the information away for an occasion just like this. He probably decided that with you out of the house it would be a good time to sneak off and go exploring on the land his granddaddy had been telling him about."

"I'm sorry," Leesa whispered again. "I should have been paying closer attention."

"Don't you worry about it, princess," Wilkie said. "A boy intent on mischief will always find some way of getting into it. Isn't that right, Chance?"

"You bet." He glanced at Jenny. "You willing to ride with me to look for him?"

"Of course."

"Wilkie, can we borrow a couple of horses?"

"You bet. I'll come, too. I can show you the direction he's likely to have gone in."

"Can I help?" Leesa asked. "Please? I have to do something."

"No, you stay here in case he calls or turns up," her uncle said. "I'll stick the cell phone in my pocket so you can reach us if something happens here. You might want to call your mama and tell her what's going on so she won't worry if you're late getting back home. Tell her I'll bring you as soon as we find the boy."

The teenager looked disappointed at not being included in the search party, but she nodded. "Should I wait in his house or yours, Uncle Wilkie?"

Wilkie glanced at Chance, who nodded. "You go on back to Chance's and stay there until you hear from us."

"I'll call White Pines," Jenny said. "Daddy and Cody can round up a few men to start searching."

"Thanks," Chance said, surprised once more by the realization that his uncle probably wouldn't hesitate to offer assistance, despite their strained relationship.

"We've only got a couple of hours before dark," Wilkie said when they'd all saddled up and mounted. "We're going to have to spread out so we can cover more ground in a hurry."

They rode over Wilkie's land toward the White Pines property line in silence. Chance was lost in thought, trying to imagine what his son had been thinking. It wasn't all that difficult to figure out really. Petey had been wanting to see White Pines. Chance had forbidden it. So, angry at his father already, he'd taken the first chance he had and gone exploring.

Chance doubted Petey would care all that much about the land or even the herds of cattle. He'd be far more interested in the house.

"Wilkie, did you specifically point the way toward the house from here?" Chance asked when they reached the fence dividing the property.

"Sure did," he said, then grinned. "I reckon the boy had a million questions about it, too. He asked if I'd ever been inside. Then he wanted to know what every single room looked like and how many outbuildings there were. Wouldn't be at all surprised if he didn't go home and map it out for himself, he was that fascinated by it."

Exactly what Chance had suspected. "Jenny, let your father know that Petey is probably peeking in his windows about now or trying to slip in the back door."

She looked over at him, then chuckled. "I'll bet you're right. That sounds exactly like what he'd do." She borrowed Wilkie's cell phone and made the call.

While they waited for word back from White Pines, they rode at a gallop over the flat pastures. When they came to a rain-swollen stream, Jenny led them to its narrowest point and took them across.

On the other side Chance reined in his horse and glanced upstream and down at the churning water.

"Stop it," Jenny said, obviously guessing the dire direction of his thoughts. "Petey's a smart kid. He would have looked for a safe place to cross. Besides, we would have spotted some sign of him if he'd tried to cross sooner than this and run into any trouble."

Chance's hand shook as he reached for a bandanna and wiped his brow. "I want to believe that."

"Then believe it. We're going to find him safe and sound at White Pines."

"Why haven't we heard something, then? Surely your father's had a chance to look around."

"There are a lot of good hiding places," Jenny said. "Especially for a kid who doesn't want to get caught."

"I agree with Jenny," Wilkie said. "You two ride on. Keep the phone with you. Just to make certain we haven't missed something, though, I'll ride along the stream for a ways."

Chance darted a worried look at the old man. "Maybe that's what I should be doing."

"No," Wilkie said firmly. "You go where it's most likely he'll be. This is just a precaution. I'll catch up with you at White Pines."

"Thanks, Wilkie," Chance said sincerely. "This means a lot to me."

"No need to thank me. Let's just find the boy safe and sound. I'm getting right fond of that rascal myself. Never realized how much I missed having kids and grandkids of my own until I started spending a little time with your boy. Leesa and her sisters are sweet girls. Their mama sees that they're real attentive to me, but it's not the same as having a child that's your own flesh and blood. And it's sure not the same as having a boy who's up to something every second.''

"That's for sure," Chance said. "Petey's definitely up to something all the time."

As Wilkie headed upstream, Chance and Jenny continued on in silence.

"It's going to be okay," she said eventually.

"I know," Chance said grimly, wishing he felt more conviction.

"We'll all laugh about it someday," she promised.

"By the time I finish with him, Petey may not feel like laughing for a very long time." He slanted a look at Jenny and saw she was smiling. "I mean it," he insisted.

"I'm sure you do," she said, "now."

Chance ignored her skepticism. "Is there anywhere between here and the house he could hide?"

"No," she said with certainty. "Cody's place is in the other direction. There's not a line shack for miles. I'll lay odds he's already somewhere around the main house. If he is, Daddy or Cody will find him."

Right on cue, the cell phone rang. "Yes," Chance said tersely.

"Son, your boy's here," Harlan Adams said.

"Found him poking around outside the stable trying to find a place to hide that horse of Wilkie's. He's fine. Good little cowboy, too. He saw to it his horse was fed and watered."

"Don't let him out of your sight," Chance muttered.

His uncle chuckled. "Not much chance of that. He's been pestering me with questions since he walked in the door. Soon as I get off the phone, the boy wants a top-to-bottom tour of the house."

Chance laughed, despite himself. "Watch the silverware. I wouldn't put anything past him."

"Don't you worry. I've got my eye on him."

Chance clicked the phone off and uttered a heartfelt sigh of relief.

"He's there?" Jenny asked.

"Oh, yes, and taking over, from what I gather."

"He's in good hands. Daddy's had a lot of experience with out-of-control kids."

"All those sons of his, huh?"

"Actually I was thinking about me," she admitted. "Remind me to tell you sometime about how we met."

"Tell me now," he said.

She shook her head. "Not now," she said, spurring her horse to a gallop. "I want to get to White Pines and see who's in charge."

A few months ago, even a few days ago, Chance would have said there'd be no doubt. His power-hungry uncle would never cede control to another living soul. Today's events had shaken his beliefs more than a little. For the second time since morning, he was wondering just how far his daddy had stretched the truth about what had happened all those years ago.

Jenny had seen the genuine worry etched in Chance's face while they'd searched for Petey. From the moment Wilkie had told them of Petey's questions about White Pines, she'd been less concerned, even though she knew there was a lot of room for mishaps along the route Petey had most likely taken.

Now, knowing that the boy was safely ensconced in her home with her father, she couldn't help thinking about Chance's earlier proposal. If she accepted, in no time at all Petey would be her full-time responsibility, too. Could she cope with him? Her experience with trying to control him in a classroom wasn't especially reassuring.

Far more important, though, could she deal with his father?

Riding hard after tossing that taunt at Chance, she could almost believe that the future would take care of itself. The rush of air washed the cobwebs out of her head and left her thinking more clearly. She would be able to talk Chance out of this insanity. He just needed some time to see how ridiculous a marriage between them would be.

In fact, his first clue was likely to appear any minute. She doubted Petey was going to react favorably to her arrival at White Pines. Surely one look at the two of them together would convince Chance that she was not mother material. He already had plenty of evidence of her inabilities in the classroom. All together, it ought to be enough to doom a relationship that had no business getting off the ground in the first place.

Feeling more confident, she slowed her horse as they approached the house. One of the stablehands was waiting. "I'll take care of the horses, miss. We'll trailer 'em back over to Wilkie's once he turns up."

"Thanks, Roddy. He shouldn't be too far behind us. He was going to ride downstream for a bit, then head this way."

Without a word Chance handed over the reins to his horse and bolted past her to the house. He didn't bother knocking. He just opened the front door and dashed inside. She followed at a more leisurely pace. She could hear the bursts of childish laughter even before she crossed the threshold. Obviously Petey was totally unaware or unconcerned that he was about to be at the center of a big-time fuss.

She found Chance standing at the doorway into the kitchen, mouth gaping. She slipped up beside him and peered inside.

Petey and her father were seated at the kitchen table, huge sundaes in front of them. They'd been topped with hot fudge, nuts and a mountain of whipped cream. Obviously neither Maritza nor her mother were at home, or her father would never have attempted sneaking such a high-cholesterol snack.

"Enjoying yourselves?" she asked wryly, drawing a guilty look from her father and a disgusted one from Petey.

"I thought you weren't home," the boy said accusingly as if she'd deliberately arrived just to spoil his fun. Before she could respond to that, he caught sight of his father and the color washed out of his face. "Uh-oh," he murmured.

Chance scowled. "I hope you have a whole lot more to say than uh-oh."

Petey glanced up at his great-uncle. "He's gonna kill me."

Harlan nodded, his expression bland. "That would be my guess."

"Aren't you gonna stop him?"

"I never interfere in matters between a father and his son," he claimed piously.

Jenny gave a snort of disbelief at that. Her father interfered in whatever struck his fancy. He shot her a warning look, however, that suggested she consider keeping her big mouth shut.

"Let's go, son," Chance said. "Now."

"But I haven't finished my sundae," Petey protested.

"I said now," Chance repeated emphatically. He glanced at Jenny. "Can we get somebody to drive us all back to my place so you can get your car?"

"Roddy will take us when he takes the horses," Jenny said. "As soon as Wilkie turns up."

"Wilkie's looking for me, too?" Petey asked worriedly. "How come?"

"Because you took off without telling anyone where you were headed," Chance informed him. "Leesa's half out of her mind with worry." He turned to Jenny. "Can I use a phone? I should give her a call."

"There's one on the counter over there." She pointed to it just as Wilkie walked in. He took one look at the melting sundaes in front of Petey and her father and sat down at the table.

"How 'bout fixing me up one of those? Missed my dinner riding all over the countryside."

Jenny got the distinct impression he wouldn't be budging until he had one. Her father started to get up, but she put a hand on his shoulder. "I'll do it." As Chance returned from making the phone call to Leesa, she said to him, "Wilkie wants a sundae. How about you?"

"This isn't a blasted ice-cream social," he muttered.

"Try telling Wilkie that."

Chance sighed. "Okay, okay, fix me one, too."

"Extra hot fudge, I'll bet."

He hesitated, then winked. "Make it extra whipped cream," he said, lowering his voice. "I've always thought there was something downright sensual about whipped cream."

Jenny trembled at the images he'd deliberately evoked. She'd wanted him distracted for a moment from his fury with Petey, but she hadn't intended that he focus his attention on her.

She turned her back on him and pulled the half-gallon of ice cream from the freezer. She was dishing scoops into three more bowls when Lizzy came in. She halted in the doorway and surveyed the scene before her, her gaze locked with Jenny's.

"Is this a celebration?" she asked cautiously.

Jenny knew exactly the sort of celebration Lizzy thought it might be. "Sure," she said hurriedly. "We're celebrating finding Petey safe and sound."

Lizzy nodded slowly. "I see. Nothing else?"

Jenny scowled at her sister. "Nothing," she said firmly.

Chance chuckled. "Come on, darlin'. Now that everybody's here, you might as well spill the news."

"What news?" her father said eagerly. "You two have something you want to tell the rest of us?"

"No," Jenny said flatly just as Chance said, "Yes."

"Well, which is it?" Wilkie asked.

"This is not a good time to get into it," Jenny said with a meaningful glance in Petey's direction.

Chance looked disappointed, but he backed off. "I suppose you're right. It can wait."

Petey regarded them both suspiciously. "What's going on?"

"Nothing that needs to concern you right now," Chance said. "In fact, if I were you, I'd be concentrating on coming up with an explanation for your behavior that'll keep me from grounding you until you graduate from high school."

Petey turned a sly look at his great-uncle. "Maybe you'd better let me move in here," he said. "I don't think it's gonna be safe for me to go home."

"Oh, I imagine you'll be safe enough," Harlan said. "But if you ever get released from your grounding, maybe your dad will let you come back to spend the night in your grandfather's old room."

Petey's eyes lit up. "You'd let me do that?"

"Of course I would."

"You should see it, Dad. It's really cool. It has posters of cowboys and stuff in it."

Jenny regarded her father with surprise. "I've never seen a room like that here." Then the explanation dawned on her. "That's the room on the third floor we were never allowed to go into, isn't it?"

Her father looked uncomfortable. "I kept it the way Hank left it. Mama tried and tried to get him to stay in one of the larger rooms on the second floor with the rest of us, but he liked being way up high. Said the housekeeper didn't like to climb all the way up there, so she never messed with his things."

Jenny heard the catch in his voice and wondered if Chance did. "You never stopped regretting that he left, did you?" she asked quietly just to be sure Chance got the message.

Her father shook his head. "In the back of my mind I suppose I was hoping that one day he'd come home again."

Jenny did glance at Chance then and saw that his hand shook as he put his spoon back on the table.

"It's time to go," he said tersely.

This time when he stood up and moved toward the door, no one argued.

Chapter Ten

Back at Wilkie's Chance saw to it that Petey apologized for worrying Leesa and then went straight to his room. Once he was assured Petey was settled in for the night, he walked Jenny to her car.

"Don't be too rough on him tomorrow," she said.

"Now that's surprising advice coming from you," he said. "I expected you to be praying I'd hog-tie him and set him up for home schooling."

A flash of humor lit her eyes. "Yes, well, that is a thought."

Her expression sympathetic, she reached up and almost put her hand on his cheek. Chance felt his heart go still as he waited for the caress that never came. She was about to pull away, when he captured her hand in his and placed it against his jaw. The reluctant touch soothed him even as it set his blood on fire.

"You'll be okay driving home?" he asked more to keep her with him than because of worry she wouldn't be perfectly safe. For reasons he hadn't had time to examine too closely, he liked being around her. It must just be the sexual attraction, he thought as she grinned and his entire body reacted.

"Chance, I've been driving these roads longer than you can possibly imagine," she assured him.

His gaze narrowed suspiciously at her amused tone. "Meaning?"

She winked at him. "I think I'll let you ponder that for a while."

"I'd stand here and try to wrangle it out of you, but I have to go in and make sure Petey is staying where I left him," he said with regret.

"I know."

"See you tomorrow?" he asked impulsively, uncertain why Monday's planned dinner suddenly seemed way too far away.

"I don't think so. We have church in the morning. The whole family comes afterward for dinner." She hesitated, then said, "You and Petey could come, too."

Chance thought about it. It would ease the family into the possibility that there was a relationship growing between him and Jenny, but he wasn't sure he wanted that to happen until he was certain what her answer to his proposal was going to be. Besides,

Petey didn't deserve a return visit to the ranch so soon after today's escapade.

Nor was Chance entirely certain he was ready to butt heads with Luke, Cody and Jordan. He had a feeling they were not going to be as easily won over or as trusting as Harlan Adams appeared to be.

"Another time," he said eventually. "But you and I have a date for Monday night. Don't forget."

"I'm not likely to," she said dryly, then regarded him thoughtfully. "Of course, you probably shouldn't leave Petey with another baby-sitter."

"Nice try," he said, amused by her attempt to put off giving him an answer. "Of course, you could answer me now and get your worrying over with and save me having to lock the doors and bar the windows to keep Petey inside while we're gone."

"Maybe you ought to leave him with my father, instead. He can be an impressive disciplinarian when he puts his mind to it."

"Yeah, I noticed that tonight when he and Petey were loading up on hot-fudge sundaes. You let me take care of Petey. You concentrate on planning our wedding."

"Don't get overly confident. You gave me forty-eight hours," she reminded him. "I'm taking every one of them."

He shrugged. "Suit yourself, but in the end the answer's going to be the same. You're going to say yes."

As soon as the teasing words were out of his mouth, Chance regretted them. Jenny was as stubborn as any Adams, and if the rest of them were anything like him, they hated being backed into a corner.

"Sorry," he said. "I didn't mean to push."

"Yes, you did, but it's okay. You come by it naturally. Fortunately I know how to push back."

He regarded her speculatively. "Will you push back if I get the notion into my head that I have to have a kiss before you drive off?"

Alarm flared briefly in her eyes, then shifted into something that might have been longing. He waited to see which turned up in her response.

"Try me," she suggested quietly.

Oddly shaken by her acquiescence, Chance didn't give her time to change her mind. He drew her at once into his arms. After taking one long, lingering look deep into her eyes, he lowered his mouth to hers. The contact sent a surge of pure adrenaline rushing through him. He was fairly certain a live wire couldn't have jolted him more.

Then Jenny was melting against him, molding her body to his and making soft little whimpering sounds in her throat. With her here in his arms, there wasn't a doubt in his mind that she wanted him as desperately as he wanted her. Every time he let her go, though, rational thought intruded, certainly for her, and, more often than not, for him.

What was he doing? The barrier between them, the one that history dictated, was growing indistinct. His proposal had been totally impulsive, an instantaneous reaction to his body's need and his obsession for White Pines. It was an incendiary combination.

He had always wondered exactly how he was going to manage to stake his claim on the ranch. This afternoon the answer had come to him like a bolt from the blue. If even so much as an acre of that land was destined to be Jenny's, then he was going to claim her—and the land right along with her.

What worried him was the increasingly distinct and totally unexpected possibility that he wasn't going to come through this maneuver unscathed. She was staking a tight-gripped claim on his heart at the same time.

No sooner had Jenny walked in the front door of White Pines after leaving Chance than whirlwind Lizzy confronted her with a barrage of questions that proved she'd inherited their mother's interrogating skills. Apparently, though, Lizzy at least kept her word about remaining silent about the possibility of Jenny's marrying Chance. Otherwise their mother would have been blasting Jenny with her share of questions.

"Would you mind telling me what the heck is going on?" her sister demanded.

Jenny deliberately misunderstood the question. "Petey ran away, he turned up here and we just took him home," she replied blandly. "Now I'm back. You knew most of that, so why are you asking?"

Lizzy impatiently waved off the evasive response. "Not that. What about this engagement?"

Jenny sighed. "Not now, please. You know the basics. That'll have to satisfy your curiosity. I'm tired. I'm going to bed."

"Not until we talk. This isn't just idle curiosity," her sister retorted. "A lot's at stake for all of us."

Her chin was jutting and her eyes were flashing with determination. She might be only twenty, but she had a highly developed stubborn streak. In fact, evidence suggested she might be the most willful Adams yet, which was a very scary thought. It ought to have the men in Los Piños, maybe even in all of Texas, trembling in their boots, especially a certain rancher named Hank Robbins. Lizzy had eyes for him and she always got what she went after.

"Lizzy, please. Can't it wait?" Jenny pleaded.

"Until when?" Lizzy countered. "You can't drop a bombshell like you did and then wave it off as inconsequential. Do you expect me to sit back and wait until you make an announcement to the whole family? Somebody has to try and talk some sense into you. Either you listen to me or I'll call Dani and Sharon Lynn and get them involved. We'll gang up on you."

That threat was enough to force Jenny to detour into the living room. She sank onto a chair and held up her hands in a gesture of surrender. "Please, leave them out of it, at least for the time being."

"Okay, fine," Lizzy agreed. "Then you can talk to me. What on earth do you think Daddy's going to say if you suddenly tell him you're going to marry Chance Adams?"

"First of all I haven't given Chance a definite answer yet. Second I have no idea what Daddy's going to say." Jenny rubbed her temples where a throbbing headache was making its presence felt. "He's unpredictable at the best of times. You saw the two of them tonight, along with Petey. Didn't it strike you that they're only a minute or two away from being thick as thieves?"

Lizzy hesitated, her expression thoughtful. "Daddy did seem to accept the two of them, didn't he?"

"Accept them? He practically invited them to move in. Maybe he figures with a couple more guys around the house, the odds will shift back in his favor and he'll get to sneak in a few more snacks."

"Not if Mama and Maritza ever find out about tonight," Lizzy said dryly. "They'll padlock the refrigerator." Her gaze narrowed. "How did we get away from this marriage business? What exactly happened after Daddy and I rode off and left the two of you? Don't leave out any of the details, either. I'd have laid odds you were going to throttle each other, not get all lovey-dovey."

"That would have been my choice," Jenny admitted. "Chance had other ideas."

"Details," Lizzy reminded her.

"Are you sure you're not just being nosy?"

"Jenny!"

"Okay, okay. We were talking and then, out of nowhere, he asked me to marry him. It's as simple as that." And as complicated, Jenny thought. She knew the proposal had nothing to do with love and everything to do with a backdoor way for Chance to get exactly what he wanted.

Unfortunately she could also see that it was the safest way to ensure that he caused her father the least amount of stress. She couldn't tell Lizzy or anyone else any of that. If she agreed to this idiotic scheme, everyone had to believe it was because she'd fallen head over heels in love with the man. Just thinking of the lies she was going to have to tell made her headache throb harder.

"Jenny, what is it?" Lizzy asked worriedly.

Jenny managed a smile. There was no point in upsetting her sister, an idealistic young woman who still had stars in her eyes when it came to romance.

"Nothing," she assured Lizzy.

"It doesn't look like nothing," her sister insisted. "A marriage proposal, especially from a certified hunk like Chance Adams, ought to make you deliriously happy. I've never seen you look sadder."

And possibly wiser, Jenny thought. In all of her thirty-five years she had never once fallen madly in love. Now when her skittering pulse told her she might be on the verge of it, the man turned out to be one who could never truly love her back.

Jenny hadn't slept a wink the past two nights. Sunday, with all the family gathered around and bursting with questions about Chance and Petey, had been filled with tension. She was so on edge she was afraid her nerves would snap like old rubber bands.

Nor could she manage to concentrate for more than a minute at a time in class on Monday. Naturally the kids spotted the weakness right away and set out to exploit it. She'd lost all semblance of control by lunchtime.

Fortunately one of the other teachers was scheduled to supervise the cafeteria. Jenny, however, refused to subject her to these pint-size terrors. They were going to be on their best behavior or she was going to quit her job and find a cabin in the wilderness to hide out in until she could restore her self-respect. Preferably it would be a cabin that Chance would never in a million years be able to find.

Clinging to her sanity by a thread, she looked at the restless students and managed to demand quiet in a tone that suggested a definite lack of tolerance for disobedience. It took several minutes, but they eventually settled down.

She regarded them evenly. "If I so much as hear a whisper about any of you misbehaving during lunch," she said quietly, "you'll have enough homework this week to keep you glued to your books at home until bedtime. Got it?"

"Yes, ma'am," Felicity said dutifully.

"Oh, stuff a sock in it," Petey muttered to the little redhead.

"Yeah, stuff a sock in it," several others chimed in.

Jenny sincerely wanted to echo the thought, but

it would set a very bad example, one that would more than likely be dutifully reported to Felicity's father, the principal from hell.

Instead, she said mildly, "We're not getting off to a very good start here." She directed a stern look straight at Petey, who turned red, but remained silent.

"That's better. Petey, why don't you lead the line to the cafeteria?"

"Huh?" He stared at her, clearly amazed that he was being chosen for this important role.

She stood up and moved to the door. "Right here, okay?"

He glanced at Timmy McPherson, who was making faces, but he eventually joined her. She nodded. "Good. Now everyone else. A nice straight line, if you please. Timmy, you be last so you can make sure everyone is together."

That ought to keep enough distance between her two worst troublemakers, she thought, pleased with the ingenuity of her plan.

She actually managed to get them into the cafeteria without further mishap. When they were all settled at tables, she turned to Megan Richards, the sixth-grade teacher. "They're all yours."

Megan chuckled. "You sound relieved. Bad morning?"

"You'll never know how bad."

"Oh, I think I will. There are some days it just doesn't pay to get out of bed."

Jenny grinned. "And some that are worse."

She spent the next half hour praying the aspirin she'd taken would kick in and relieve the headache that had started two nights before and continued unabated. Naturally the pills didn't help at all, and before she knew it she was back in the classroom with twenty-five kids who'd all had too much sugar for lunch. If she'd had the strength herself, she would have taken them for a long brisk walk to burn off a little of their energy.

Instead, she gave them a very long reading assignment and then sank into the chair behind her desk. She was so grateful for the blessed silence that followed that she let the students keep on reading until the final bell rang. Eager faces turned to her expectantly. She grinned. At least she'd accomplished one thing this year. They no longer bolted for the door at the first sound of the bell. It gave her the illusion of control. It was a reassuring way to end the day.

"You may be excused," she said, trying not to cover her ears to block out the ensuing sounds of chaos.

Everyone was gone in a matter of minutes. Except Petey, she realized, who was still lurking in the doorway.

"You'd better hurry, Petey. You'll miss your bus."

"Dad said you'd give me a ride."

Jenny stared. "He what?"

"If you don't want to or something, it's okay,"

he said a little too eagerly. "Like you said, I can still catch the bus."

What on earth was Chance up to now? Jenny wondered. He must have a reason for manipulating the two of them together like this. Maybe he wanted to ensure that Petey made it home and didn't trust him to take the bus. Or maybe he was simply hoping they'd find some way to get along. That did make sense, though she couldn't help resenting him for making the decision without consulting her. What if she'd had other plans this afternoon? What if, for instance, she'd been in a rush to get home and get ready for the most important date of her life?

"I can take you," she said, as much to prove she wasn't anxious to get dressed for the evening as anything else. "I'll just be a minute."

She gathered up the papers she intended to grade later that night after her command dinner date, along with her purse and coat, and headed for the door. Petey trailed behind her until they were well out of sight of the kids still lingering in front of the building.

"How did you enjoy visiting White Pines Saturday?" she asked when they were settled in her car.

"It's cool," Petey said, then immediately looked guilty as if he shouldn't admit he'd enjoyed himself.

"I think my dad really liked showing you around," Jenny said. "He thinks you're a pretty terrific kid."

Petey looked at her with surprise. "He said that?"

"Sure. He told me so first thing on Sunday. Besides, why wouldn't he like you?"

"I dunno. I just thought, you know, because of my granddad and everything, that he'd be mad I came over."

"Did he seem mad?"

Petey paused, his expression thoughtful. "No, not really."

"There, you see?"

"Could I ask you something?"

"Of course."

He regarded her worriedly. "Do you think my granddad would be mad that I, you know, ate ice cream there and kinda hung out with your dad?"

Jenny hesitated. "Well, I never knew your granddad, but it seems to me it's always best if people get to know each other and try to understand each other. I think he'd be proud you did that."

The concept seemed to startle Petey. "Really?"

"Absolutely. I think it was good that you came, although it might have been better if you'd had your dad's permission."

"Yeah, no kidding," Petey said. "He was really mad at me."

"Because you scared Leesa and him and all the rest of us."

He glanced at her in astonishment. "You, too?"

"Of course, me, too."

"Why?"

The question stymied Jenny. Obviously Petey was smart enough to realize he'd caused her nothing but trouble. He also knew it wasn't likely to endear him to her. "Because you are a terrific kid," she said eventually. "Even if you've done everything in your power to hide that fact from me."

"I don't get it," he said, clearly confused by her reaction. "I figured you must hate me."

"No way. I may not like some of the things you've done, but I've tried to understand why you've done them. I'm still working on that part. Maybe you could explain it to me."

"You mean like why I cut off Mary's hair?"

"Uh-huh. We could start with that."

"It was a dare, kinda." He slanted a look at her. "Pretty dumb, huh?"

"Pretty dumb," Jenny agreed.

"That's what Dad said. I did apologize, though." He made a face. "Now Mary has a crush on me."

Jenny grinned. "I noticed."

"She's been following me around and stuff and she's always asking me to do things with her, like come over to her house or go out for pizza with her mom and dad."

"Would that be so terrible? Mary seems like a nice girl."

Petey looked horrified. "But that's just it. She's a *girl*."

"Someday you'll be grateful for that," Jenny promised as they turned into the driveway at Wilkie's. She saw Chance come out of the barn and start toward them. Petey bounded out of the car and headed for the house with no more than a wave the instant the car rolled to a stop.

"He must be anxious to get to his homework," Chance said dryly.

"Or away from me," Jenny countered. "How come you didn't let him ride the bus? Were you hoping we'd get to know each other better?"

"That's one possible outcome," he agreed. "But I was also hoping it would give me a chance to catch a glimpse of you before tonight."

His heated gaze seemed to burn straight through her. "Really?" she asked, sounding disgustingly breathless.

"In fact, forget about later," he said, moving closer to the car and reaching through the window to cup her face between his hands. "I think maybe I'll just steal a kiss right now—you know, to tide me over."

Jenny decided it was way past time to show a little of her old familiar spunk. As he ducked his head in the window, she twisted just beyond his reach. His kiss landed in the air near her ear. His expression of astonishment was worth every bit of awkward maneuvering.

"You're getting just a little too full of yourself," she told him, extraordinarily pleased with herself for the first time in weeks. She'd always had gumption to spare. It was about time she demonstrated it.

Chance's gaze narrowed. "Meaning?"

"You're a bright man. Figure it out." She put the

car into gear and inched it away from him. He stared after her in openmouthed astonishment.

"I'll pick you up at six," he called after her.

Feeling downright giddy from her first tiny victory, Jenny shook her head. "I'll meet you at seven."

"Do I at least get to pick the place?" he asked, visibly irritated.

Given the amazingly limited number of choices, Jenny figured she could allow him that much. "Sure. Why not?"

"Chandler's Steak 'n' Ribs?"

That was perfect, she thought. No one in the family ever went there. They preferred their steaks from their own cattle and cooked on a backyard grill. Chandler's was forty miles away, but it boasted the only fancy meals to be had without going all the way to Fort Worth. For just an instant Jenny regretted that they wouldn't be making the trip in one car.

"Want to change your mind about going with me?" he asked as if he'd read her mind.

"I don't think so. In this part of the country, that's just around the corner," she said.

He grinned. "Suit yourself."

Jenny gave a little nod. "From now on that's exactly what I intend to do."

Chance tilted his head and regarded her quizzically. "Darlin', that almost sounds like a warning."

She grinned. "Good ear."

"You're playing with fire. You know that, don't you?"

"Of course," she said airily. "What fun is life if you're not living on the edge?"

Chance chuckled. "Don't look now, but you're about to topple over."

"Is that supposed to scare me?"

"It should."

"It doesn't. How about you?"

"Darlin', I've been flat out terrified from the minute we met."

The heartfelt admission had Jenny humming all the way to White Pines. This evening might just turn out a whole lot better than she'd anticipated.

Chapter Eleven

Something about Jenny had changed, Chance thought. It wasn't just that she'd deliberately avoided his kiss, although that had been disconcerting enough. It was her whole attitude. It had undergone a radical shift. It was as if she'd discovered she held some sort of power over him.

Had he been that transparent? Had she guessed that his feelings for her weren't based entirely on his obsession with the family ranch? Or had the implications of the obsession itself finally registered? Had she concluded that she had something he wanted and that she might as well make that work to her advantage? Maybe she knew more about power and control than he'd realized.

Whichever it was, dinner promised to be darned interesting. He was looking forward to it.

Ironically, after this afternoon he wasn't nearly as certain that the outcome would be what he'd imagined. While that would be disappointing in the short term, it presented him with an absolutely fascinating long-term challenge.

If Jenny turned him down, he'd just have to figure out another way to get what he wanted. What confused him was that he was no longer quite as sure whether that was Jenny or White Pines.

He was still trying to figure out what to make of the change in Jenny as he followed the directions Wilkie had given him to the steakhouse. After thirty minutes or so, he spotted the neon sign and turned into the huge parking lot that was already crowded with cars and a few tractor trailers, hinting that not only was the food superb, but that the atmosphere wasn't pretentious. To his way of thinking that was an ideal combination.

He glanced around the parking lot but didn't immediately spot Jenny's impractical little sports car. Disappointed, he headed toward the door to wait for her inside. Before he could get it open, though, he heard the familiar roar of her engine and the squeal of her tires as she braked none too gently less than a half-dozen spaces away from the entrance. There was absolutely nothing prim and prissy about the way the woman drove, he thought, smiling. Just more evidence of the passion churning inside her, waiting to be unleashed by the right man.

A moment later the sight of her wiped the smile off his face. In fact, it was all he could do to breathe.

When she exited the car, her legs bared by an astonishingly short skirt and emphasized by very slinky high heels, Chance's mouth gaped and his heart thundered in his chest. As desperately as he wanted to survey those long shapely legs, he also wanted to get her inside where they would be safely tucked under a table and out of view of every other male.

With her high cheekbones touched by blush and framed by wisps of black hair, and her lipstick a brighter shade than she usually wore, she was devastatingly beautiful and stunningly sexy, the kind of sexy that no twenty-year-old understood. It came with maturity and experience and confidence.

How had he ever thought of her as prim and prissy? he wondered. If someone had slapped a picture of her on a calendar, men around the world would have been panting over her.

As she walked up beside him, she patted his cheek gently. "Don't look now, but you're practically drooling," she said, then sashayed straight on past with a provocative sway of her hips.

Obviously she was aware of the effect she'd created, he thought. It appeared, in fact, that she'd worked on this new image just to unnerve him.

"What have you done to yourself?" he asked, his tone grim as he followed her, his gaze locked on her backside. He was tempted to strip off his jacket and drape it around her waist to prevent others from seeing that tempting little behind.

She glanced over her shoulder. Eyes wide, she

stared at him innocently. "It's an important night, isn't it? And this is a nice restaurant. I thought I'd dress up for the occasion."

"You barely dressed at all," he muttered, suddenly aware that the dazzling hot pink top she'd chosen to wear with that thigh-skimming skirt barely reached her waist. With every move she made an inch or more of flesh was displayed. Forget the jacket. He was sorely tempted to throw his arms around her to cover her up. Unfortunately he wasn't at all certain his motives were entirely pure. He wanted to touch that silken skin very very badly.

He was so busy fighting his own base desire that the hostess had to ask twice if they had a reservation before her question registered. He nodded mutely.

"Adams," Jenny supplied, looking highly amused.

"Oh, of course. Right this way," the woman said, looking Chance over approvingly.

He hardly noticed. Mouth dry and heart hammering, his gaze was glued to the sensual sway of Jenny's backside as she walked to the table. Women should be banned from wearing heels that high, he concluded, at least out in public. It did something to them, to the way they moved, that was downright indecent. His blood was humming so fast and furiously and he was so close to being fully aroused it was embarrassing.

"You did this on purpose, didn't you?" he demanded when the hostess had gone.

"Did what?"

"Wore that outfit."

She regarded him innocently. "I bought this outfit on my last trip to New York. I found it in a perfectly respectable department store. I've worn it before and no one's complained. What's wrong with it?"

"There's not enough of it."

Her laugh was low and throaty and sexy. Was that new, too? Had she set out to torment him tonight? If so, she was doing a fine job of it. He fingered the ring he'd tucked in his pocket and wondered if he truly had lost his mind to even consider marrying this woman. She was entirely too disconcerting. She'd keep him tied in knots.

"You look uneasy," she observed, that amused glint flashing in her eyes again.

"Do I?" He barely resisted the need to lick his suddenly parched lips.

"Is there some problem I don't know about?"

"Problem?" he echoed. "No, there's no problem." He sucked in a deep breath and deliberately opened the menu. Maybe if he focused his attention on T-bones and porterhouses, he'd regain his equilibrium.

Suddenly he felt the skim of a stocking-clad foot up his calf and almost bolted from his chair. A light sweat broke out on his brow as he tried to pretend he'd noticed nothing. The amused smirk on Jenny's face suggested that she knew exactly how she was affecting him and that she was enjoying the heck out of it.

Of all the times for the woman to discover the

power of her own sensuality, he thought despondently. As he knew all too well, power was a heady thing.

All he'd ever wanted was a simple little marriage of convenience, maybe a little revenge. There was no longer anything remotely simple about this. As for revenge, at the moment Jenny was having the last laugh.

Okay, he thought, trying to adjust to her unexpected new tactics. Two could play at this game. He was willing to bet he'd had a whole lot more experience.

He slid one hand beneath the table and reached for her thigh. He brushed a light caress from her kneecap to the hem of her skirt, all the while keeping his gaze fixed on the menu selections. Her sharp gasp and sudden shift indicated he'd made his point. Retaliation could be rather sweet, he concluded, repeating the caress just for the sheer fun of it.

"Have you found anything that appeals to you?" he inquired lightly.

She swallowed hard and avoided his gaze. Chance grinned and deliberately gave her knee a last little squeeze. Check and checkmate.

A small country band started to play just then, a provocative slow song about lost love and second chances. Chance figured the opportunity was too good to pass up. He'd managed to turn the tables and disconcert her a little. Maybe he could actually manage to recapture the edge he'd lost.

"Care to dance?"

Her gaze flew to his. Her panicky expression suggested she'd rather be buried in mud and left to swelter in the noonday sun.

"We haven't even ordered," she protested.

"There's no rush. I hate to waste a song as pretty as this one. Makes me think of slow lovin' and long nights," he whispered, his gaze locked with hers. He stood up and held out a hand. "Come on, darlin'. Let's see how you move on a dance floor."

Apparently he put a little too much challenge into his tone, because her eyes suddenly flashed fire. She slapped her hand in his and rose gracefully, slipping her foot back into her shoe before following him into the middle of the handful of couples already dancing.

With those heels on, she was only an inch or two shorter than he was. Chance slid his arms around her waist. Jenny hesitated a beat, then tucked her head into his shoulder. She looped her hands behind his neck. Her warm breath feathered against the V of bare skin where his shirt collar was open. That whisper of air stirred him as effectively as a caress.

In no time he was surrounded by the daring come-hither scent of her perfume. No rose garden had ever smelled so inviting. Her body heat beckoned to him. In a matter of seconds she was fitted to him as intimately as if they'd been carved from a single piece of wood and were destined to link up curve to curve like an interlocking puzzle.

He was no longer sure which of them had started the game or whether it even mattered. All he knew was the desperate hunger to finish it, in bed, her arms and legs wrapped tightly around him. If he'd been convinced she would agree to it, he would have made a dash for the nearest motel room and to hell with dinner. But he wasn't feeling quite that confident.

The music came to a slow sensual conclusion. For an instant Chance couldn't bring himself to release her. He had the feeling he'd just glimpsed heaven, but it was elusive yet. Another minute, maybe two, and he was all but certain it would be his.

"Chance?" she murmured.

"Hmm?"

"The music's over." There was a breathless catch in her voice.

He grinned, aware she couldn't see it. "I know."

"Shouldn't we go back to the table? People are staring."

"Don't tell me the infamous Jenny Adams is scared of being the talk of the town."

She sighed and her breath feathered against his throat. "Being talked about is the least of my concerns."

"Oh?"

She tilted her head and gazed at him innocently. "It's just that I'm getting a really desperate need to strip naked and have my way with you."

Chance fought the urge to shout, "Hallelujah!" and bolt from the restaurant with Jenny in his arms. Instead, he met her gaze and said, "If that's a genuine offer, darlin', we can be out of here before the next tune starts.''

A trace of worry skittered across her face, but she never lowered her gaze. "Without dinner?" she asked, then added in a tone usually reserved for seduction, "I'm starved."

Very brave, very cool, he thought. Only a faint tremor in her voice suggested she was at all fearful about his possible response. He grinned. This tit-for-tat banter was escalating nicely. It would be interesting to see which of them backed out of the game first. His money was on Ms. Adams. She was good, but it was clear to him she was new to the technique. He doubted she'd have the nerve to stay the course.

"Now that you mention it, sustenance is probably a good idea," he said softly, "especially if this evening's destined to end the way you've been hinting."

Turning, he kept one hand clasped firmly in his and led the way back to their table. As he seated her, he bent down and brushed a kiss across the nape of her neck. She gave a start as if he'd touched her with a branding iron.

"You're a little jumpy, darlin'. Anything wrong?"

She swallowed hard. "Not a thing," she said, her voice breathless.

"Good. I'd suggest you go for a nice big steak. That ought to tide you over till morning, no matter how much activity the night holds."

"I'll have a salad," she said, her expression defiant. "A small house salad."

"At the rate things are going, that won't sustain you through foreplay."

"It will sustain me just fine," she insisted stubbornly.

He shrugged. "Suit yourself. How about an appetizer at least? Maybe some oysters?" he suggested. "I hear they have some interesting side effects."

"Don't you ever think about anything except sex?" she muttered.

"Not when someone's signaling the way you've been tonight," he replied blandly. "Once that track's been laid down, I'm more than willing to ride it to the end." He regarded her innocently. "Unless, of course, you've been playing some sort of game here. Have you?"

"No, of course not," she said firmly.

He gave her an encouraging smile. "Good."

She met his gaze boldly. "Have you?"

"Absolutely not."

"Fine."

When their waiter came, Chance ordered a beer for himself and white wine for Jenny. While they waited for the drinks, he let the silence linger and swell. He wanted her to sit and worry about just what she'd gotten herself into. In truth he could use the time to try to figure out just how far he was going to press this game she'd started.

On a purely physical level he wanted her so badly

he ached. That much was straightforward and clearcut. On an emotional level it was a hell of a lot more complicated. Why? Because something told him that once he slept with Jenny Adams, nothing would ever be simple again.

Jenny had recognized the mistake she'd made the minute she'd seen the flare of heat in Chance's eyes as she'd walked across the parking lot. Everything that had happened since pretty much proved she had dangerously miscalculated.

All she'd intended was to throw the man off-kilter, maybe get the upper hand for the first time since they'd met. She'd planned on engaging in a little light flirtation, a little blatant seduction, maybe even indulging in a breath-stealing kiss or two just for the pure exhilaration of it.

It had stopped being fun and started throwing up very serious warning signals the minute she'd seen that avid look in his eyes. He was a whole lot better at flirtation and seduction than she was. She'd turned weak-kneed and muddle-brained the minute he'd touched her. It had required every ounce of will-power she possessed and then some to insist on having dinner, rather than racing him to the nearest bed.

And then, out of pure cussedness, she'd ordered an itty-bitty house salad. How long could it possibly take to eat a handful of lettuce leaves and a couple of cherry tomatoes? Fifteen minutes if she dragged it out? She should have ordered a half-dozen courses, starting with an appetizer and going all the way through to dessert and coffee.

Well, there was still time to insist on looking over the dessert cart. Maybe she'd order a huge bowl of fresh strawberries with whipped cream and linger over them for at least an hour. She glanced up at Chance and noted that he was watching her with his usual amused expression. Forget the whipped cream, she thought, as a vision of Chance slowly licking it off her surfaced and shot her temperature up several degrees.

"Something worrying you?" he inquired.

Jenny smiled brightly. "Not a thing." She lifted her wineglass, the only one she intended to allow herself all evening. "Nice wine."

"We should have ordered a bottle," Chance said.

"One glass is plenty. I'll nurse it."

"You've already finished all of it but the last swallow," he pointed out.

Jenny stared at the glass in astonishment. The wine was gone. She must have tossed back most of it when her throat went dry under Chance's intense scrutiny.

"Oh, well," she said with a shrug. "I guess it's water for me for the rest of the meal." She picked up her glass and drained it, then glanced around desperately for a waitress to refill it with lots and lots of ice.

"You're sure?" he asked.

"Absolutely. I never drink more than one when I'm driving."

He nodded. "Smart thinking. Too bad we didn't come together. Then I could be the designated driver. Maybe, though, if you had another glass of wine, you'd relax."

Relax? No way. In fact, Jenny thought, coming separately might have been the one bright decision she'd made all day. Surely whatever amorous notions either of them entertained would die out on the long lonely drive back home. That was her safety net, her one guarantee that no matter how far she went flirting, she could get home without giving in to his lust and her increasingly persistent hormones.

He sat back in his chair and observed her with that all-too-familiar irritatingly smug expression. Jenny resisted the urge to squirm.

"Okay," she finally said. "Just spit it out."

"What?"

"Whatever's on your mind. You're the one who insisted on getting together for dinner."

"And you're the one who was supposed to come prepared to answer a question," he reminded her. "Have you thought about it?"

Jenny decided to be deliberately dense. She'd thought about his proposal until her head was spinning. She hadn't come up with an answer she could live with, not without feeling as if she was betraying someone, either her family or herself.

"What question?" she asked.

He shook his head, his expression sorrowful. "Oh, darlin, you can do better than that."

"No," she said stubbornly. "I think you ought to

repeat the question just so I'm sure you haven't changed your mind or something. Spell out all the terms so we're clear on what sort of arrangement you're making."

"Arrangement? I suppose that's one word for it," he said. "Okay. Whatever you say, darlin'."

Before she realized what he intended, he was out of his chair and down on one knee next to her. He had a small jewelry box in one hand. When he flipped open the lid, the most gorgeous diamond ring she'd ever seen was displayed. The sight of its glittering beauty took her breath away. The implication of it left her speechless. She had never really expected him to carry things this far. She'd all but convinced herself he'd been teasing her.

She sighed at the folly of her thinking. That ring was no joke.

"Jenny Adams, will you marry me?" he asked loudly enough to draw attention.

Jenny could feel at least a dozen pairs of eyes turn toward the two of them expectantly. Silence fell in their corner of the restaurant. She wasn't absolutely certain, but she was relatively confident this was the most humiliating moment of her life. She'd been at the center of a fair amount of gossip over the years, but this scene promised to be the story that lingered.

"Get up," she hissed under her breath.

"Not until you give me an answer."

"Please," she begged.

"Only if you take the ring and try it on," he said.

"That's blackmail."

He grinned. "Yep. As you've reminded me more than once, I'm good at it."

Jenny debated doing absolutely nothing and seeing how long Chance would stay right where he was. This had to be humiliating for him, too.

Apparently not, she realized when he still hadn't budged a couple of minutes later. Unfortunately she wasn't made of the same stuff. The attention from all the other diners was way too embarrassing. She wanted to get this farce over with. Her left hand trembled, but she held it out.

Chance took the ring out of the box and slowly slid it onto her finger. The contrast of cool metal and his warm skin set off gooseflesh. His gaze locked with hers and she found she couldn't quite bring herself to look away. Chance, however, did. He gazed at the ring, which sparkled brightly even in the dimly lit restaurant.

"A perfect fit," he murmured.

Jenny choked back a bubble of panic deep in her throat and followed the direction of his gaze. The ring was spectacular and fit as if it had been made for her hand. She recalled how many times as a girl she'd taken out the engagement ring her mother had put away after her divorce from Jenny's father. She had slipped it on and imagined the day when she would have a ring of her own, given to her by a man who worshiped her. Now that moment was here, and the man cared more about her prospective inheritance than he did about her. Rather than the ecstasy she'd once imagined feeling, she wanted to cry.

Before she could make a complete fool of herself by bursting into tears, everyone surrounding them assumed that her decision had been given. They all broke into applause. A bottle of champagne arrived at the table, a gift from the management. Jenny felt like the worst kind of fraud, but at least Chance made good on his promise. He went back to his seat. He just didn't release her hand. For some reason, the warmth of his grip felt reassuring.

Now that she'd gotten her way, Jenny was almost tempted to rip the ring from her finger before she became too comfortable wearing it. Something in Chance's expression stopped her. He looked almost shaken, as if he, too, was being torn by unexpected emotions.

"Don't take it off," he said quietly as if he'd guessed her intentions.

"Chance—"

"Please. Think it over at least."

"I've *been* thinking it over."

"Doesn't the fact that you couldn't say no outright tell you something?"

"It tells me that I love my family, that I would do almost anything in the world to prevent them from being hurt." Her voice broke as she again fought back tears.

"Is that all?" he asked doubtfully.

She stared back at him defiantly. "What else could it be?"

"Maybe, just maybe, there's a part of you that wants to marry me for your own sake."

"Marry a man who's blackmailing me?" she asked incredulously. "You must be crazy."

"I don't think so. The attraction's there, darlin'. If you're honest with yourself, you can't deny it."

"Attraction's not a reason to get married. Attraction can burn itself out way too fast."

"You want love, then? I'm surprised. I didn't peg you as a romantic."

"Every woman's a romantic."

"I don't know. I've met a few who were driven more by ambition and greed. Their matches weren't made in heaven. They were mergers. That's what ours could be. We'd be great partners, Jenny."

Her heart sank at the cool assessment of their future, the bland definition of their relationship. She didn't want a partner, at least not a business partner. She wanted a man in her life who loved her. She wanted passion and excitement.

Chance could give her the passion. She had very little doubt about that, but would it be enough if there was no love behind it? No matter how desperately she wanted to help her family, she couldn't compromise on that. Deep in her heart, she knew her father would understand and forgive her.

She took one last longing look at the ring Chance had given her, then slowly twisted it off and held it out in the palm of her hand. "I can't accept it," she said quietly.

"Not even to save White Pines," he said, clearly stunned.

With tears in her eyes she shook her head. "God help me, not even for that."

Chapter Twelve

Chance watched in stunned silence as Jenny picked up her purse and left the steakhouse. One part of him wanted desperately to stop her. Another part told him he'd escaped disaster by the skin of his teeth. The contrary forces kept him immobilized as she walked away.

"Sir, is there anything I can get you?" the waitress inquired solicitously. Her tone held just a hint that she could cure all his ills.

Chance tried to work up some enthusiasm for that possibility, but he couldn't. Mindless mutually satisfying sex wasn't the answer to what ailed him. Nor was alcohol, though he did gaze longingly at the row of liquor bottles behind the bar.

"Just the check," he told the obviously disappointed waitress. He read her name tag for the first time. "Thanks, Thelma."

"You bet, handsome. If you change your mind, let me know. I know all about making a man feel better."

Responding automatically, Chance grinned. "I'll bet you do, sweetheart, but it would be wasted on me tonight."

Thelma left and returned in minutes with his check, then asked, "Mind if I give you some advice?"

Chance figured he was at such a low point he'd take advice from wherever it came. "Go right ahead."

"Forget about her. She looks a little stuck-up to me, like she's better than the rest of us."

Chance thought about Jenny turning down marriage and a chance to save her family's ranch, all because she still believed in the happily-ever-after kind of love.

"Maybe she is," he said quietly.

Maybe his priorities were the ones that were all messed up. There'd been a time when he'd been lucky enough to love a woman and have her love him back, heart and soul. With his beloved Mary he'd known the joy of that kind of marriage first-hand. What kind of man would trade that for a piece of land he'd never set eyes on until a few months back? What kind of man expected a woman to sacrifice such deep emotions? He wasn't crazy about the answer that came to him.

He tossed a handful of bills on the table. "See you," he said to Thelma as he slid away from the table.

"Anytime, lover. You know where to find me."

Chance appreciated the invitation, but he knew he'd never take her up on it. Unfortunately the woman who'd taken him totally by surprise and managed to get under his skin had just walked out on him. And he had some long hard thinking to do before he made up his mind what—if anything—to do about it.

"How was your date with Chance?" Lizzy demanded before Jenny was even through the front door.

Jenny frowned. She really didn't want to do a postmortem of the evening, not with her curious younger sister. She didn't want advice or pity or sympathy. She didn't want to have to explain her decision, not when she wasn't entirely sure she understood it herself.

"Were you waiting up for me?" she asked testily. "Don't you have better things to do?"

"Who's waiting up?" Lizzy retorted, instantly defensive. "It's barely ten o'clock." She studied Jenny worriedly. "Didn't it go well? Did you two fight? Or did you finally come to your senses?"

Jenny thought back over the evening, from its promising, even stimulating beginning, all the way to the disastrous ending when she had made her decision and walked out on Chance. She could still remember the way that diamond ring had felt on her finger and the husky note in Chance's voice when he'd slid it on. If only...

She brought herself up short. There were no *if onlys* here. Chance wanted White Pines, not her, and she wasn't about to become a pawn in his game. That was that. Sooner or later she would have to tell her father what had happened. She would have to warn him that Chance might be more vindictive than ever since she'd thwarted his scheme.

Just not tonight. Tonight she didn't want to think any more about Chance Adams at all. She wanted to sink into the oblivion of sleep. Maybe if she slept deeply enough, she wouldn't dream about the promise and hope that ring could have represented if their lives had been different and both their last names hadn't been Adams.

"I'm going to bed," she told Lizzy.

"But—"

"Good night," Jenny said firmly. "I'll see you tomorrow."

Lizzy seemed about to protest, but Jenny's expression must have warned her to save it. Instead, she pulled Jenny into a fierce hug.

"I love you. Remember that. And so does everyone else in the family. It's not up to you to save us all by yourself. It never has been."

Jenny smiled wanly. "I know." She only wondered how sorely tested that love was going to be when the others learned the truth about what she'd done tonight, when they realized she could have protected White Pines and hadn't done so.

Jenny hadn't thought it possible, but Tuesday turned out to be an even worse nightmare than Monday had been. Petey was so completely out of control, so totally defiant, that by noon she'd marched him down to the principal's office and left him there, ignoring Patrick Jackson's expression of triumph. Obviously the principal was pleased she'd lost control again.

Petey looked slightly chagrined when she went to get him after lunch. In fact, he even apologized, albeit halfheartedly.

"I didn't mean to make Felicity cry," he told her as they walked back to the classroom together. "But she's such a little suck-up." He slanted a look at Jenny. "I told Mr. Jackson that, too. I guess I sort of forgot he's her dad. I thought for sure he was gonna have a stroke."

Jenny had to work very hard not to laugh. "I can imagine," she said.

Jenny actually shared Petey's opinion of Felicity, but that didn't excuse Petey's tormenting the child earlier by stealing her homework and making all her answers incorrect. Felicity, who prided herself on her neatness, had been humiliated not just by the inexplicable mistakes on her papers, but by the sloppiness of the work. She'd been in tears when Jenny had insisted she hand the paper in or get an *F* on the assignment.

One look at the messy work and Jenny had guessed what had happened. One look at Petey's smug expression and Timmy McPherson's triumphant one had confirmed it. Getting Petey to admit he was responsible had been traumatic for all the students, every one of whom she'd threatened with detention if someone didn't confess.

She glanced at Petey. "Why did you do it? I don't want to hear that stuff about Felicity being a teacher's pet. I can see why that might make her an easy target. Why did you feel that you had to do something you knew I would punish you for?"

"I dunno," he whispered, looking miserable.

"I don't buy that. Come on, Petey. Tell me why. Did this have something to do with Timmy again?"

"No."

"What, then?"

He sighed heavily. "Do I have to tell?"

"Yes," she said firmly. "I want the whole truth this time."

"I guess it's because you pay attention to me when I do stuff," he said, avoiding her gaze.

She stared at him incredulously. "Petey, I'd pay attention to you if you were good, too."

"But you wouldn't come to the house and stuff."

"I'm confused. I thought you didn't like me coming around. I thought you didn't like me at all because of who I am."

"That was before."

"Before what?"

"Before I figured out you were kinda okay and

you made Dad laugh sometimes, the way he used to.''

Jenny saw that for the supreme compliment it was. Coming from Petey, who'd been raised to dislike anyone connected to Harlan Adams, it was high praise, indeed. As for her ability to make Chance smile, that was yesterday's news, but apparently Petey didn't know it yet.

"I'm glad you think I'm okay," she said quietly. "I think you're pretty okay, too." She regarded him soberly. "But I'd like you even more if you'd stop doing these terrible things to your classmates just to get my attention."

"But I want you to keep coming to the house. I think Dad does, too."

"I'm not so sure about that," Jenny protested. In fact, she was fairly confident she wouldn't be seeing any more of Chance Adams than was absolutely necessary from now on. "Look, maybe you and I can get a soda at Dolan's after school once in a while. Or maybe you can come over to White Pines and go riding with me."

His eyes widened and he gazed at her hopefully. "Really?"

"I'll try to work it out. I promise." She stared at him intently. "But only if you're on your best behavior in class from now on, okay?"

He grinned. "Okay." He raised his hand to give her a high five.

"Since we're on a roll here," she said, "maybe you should work on getting those grades up, too.

You're a whole lot smarter than you've been letting on."

He shrugged. "Maybe a little."

Jenny chuckled. "*A*'s and *B*'s. I won't settle for anything less."

"Okay, okay. You're worse than Dad. It's way too much pressure for a little kid like me."

"Oh, I think you can handle it," she said with confidence. After all, he'd just manipulated her into doing exactly what he'd wanted. He had those Adams genes in spades.

As they reached the door to the classroom, Petey hung back. "Can I ask you something? It's something I can't really talk to my dad about."

"Of course," she said at once. His tone alerted her that whatever was on his mind was something very serious to him. "But I'll bet you could talk to your dad about it if you wanted to. He cares about you, Petey. You know that."

"I know. It's just that this is about Mom, and sometimes talking about her makes him real sad."

Jenny's heart seemed to stop. She'd never considered that Chance might still harbor feelings for the wife he'd lost two years earlier. "What about your mom?" she asked quietly.

Petey gazed up at her with tear-filled eyes. "Do you think it's terrible that sometimes it's real hard for me to remember her?"

Jenny knelt down and gathered him close, oblivious to the possibility that someone might come along and see her comforting one of her students, especially one she'd banished to the principal's office only a couple of hours earlier.

"Oh, sweetie, it's perfectly normal to forget sometimes. You were very young when she died."

"But she was my mom," he protested. "I should remember what she looked like and not have to stare at some old picture to get it right."

"I know." She tapped the center of his chest gently. "I'll bet you never forget the way you felt about her right here, in your heart."

His expression brightened a little. "Yeah," he said slowly. "That's true."

"It's not the details that are important, not the color of her eyes or the shape of her nose, but the times you shared and the way she made you feel. Those memories will never go away."

Petey regarded her worriedly. "Not even if I got a new mom someday?"

Jenny grinned and tried not to turn weepy at the realization that she wouldn't be that new mom. "Not even then," she assured him.

His expression turned sly. "Then I guess I'll tell Dad it's okay if he decides to marry you."

Jenny winced. The kid truly did have lousy timing. "Maybe you'd better not tell him that just now."

"How come? I think he wants to."

What the heck was she supposed to do now? she wondered. Tell him she'd turned down his father's proposal? That was news best delivered by Chance.

She suspected he was going to be stunned that Petey had even been thinking along those lines.

"Sweetie, marriage is a very grown-up decision," she explained. "Maybe you'd better just leave that up to your dad."

"Are you sure? Sometimes he can be real mule-headed about stuff. At least that's what Grandpa used to say. He said when Dad gets that way, he needs a good shove."

"I doubt he meant for you to do the shoving," Jenny said. "Now let's get back to class, okay?"

"Yeah, I guess."

Jenny grinned. "You don't have to sound so over-joyed about it."

"Hey," he said, "it's school. I'm a kid. What do you expect?"

Jenny sighed. There were days, she was forced to concede, when she felt pretty much the same way.

Still, it had been a good conversation, if ever so slightly disconcerting. In fact, her relationship with Chance aside, she'd begun to feel fairly hopeful about life in general by the time she drove home that afternoon.

The feeling didn't last. The sight of all the cars and trucks in front of the house brought her spirits crashing right back down. Something was wrong if everyone in the family had turned up in the middle of the afternoon on a weekday.

Jenny took the front steps two at a time and burst into the living room where everyone was gathered, their expressions as somber as if a major illness had struck.

"Daddy?" she asked at once. "Is he—"

"I'm just fine, darlin' girl," he said quietly, coming up behind her and giving her shoulder a squeeze. "I was just in the kitchen getting something to drink. It's the rest of 'em. They've all got their feathers ruffled."

Relief washed over her, only to vanish as she studied the somber faces in the living room. "What now?" she asked.

To her surprise it was her mother who answered.

"I had a call today from an attorney in Dallas, a big-shot partner at a firm with a dozen names on the masthead," Janet said.

Jenny felt her stomach clench. Only one piece of legal business she could think of would draw everyone in the family together on the spur of the moment. "About?" she asked reluctantly.

"That mean-spirited snake of a cousin of ours is suing for half of White Pines," Cody snapped.

Jenny reached for the back of a chair to brace herself. He couldn't have. It hadn't even been twenty-four hours since she'd turned down his marriage proposal. Had he made all the arrangements ahead of time just in case she said no? Or had he planned to do it all along no matter what she said? Maybe he'd just been playing a sick game with her.

"Damn him," she muttered.

"My sentiments exactly," Luke chimed in bitterly. "I don't know where the hell he gets off waltzing into town after all these years and stirring up trouble.''

"Maybe if you all had done the thinking I asked you to do and settled on a solution, it wouldn't have come to this,'' her father said quietly.

Jenny swallowed hard and said, "I could have stopped it. I'm sorry.'' With that she burst into tears and ran from the room, leaving everyone except Lizzy gaping after her.

"I'll talk to her,'' Janet said.

Jenny heard her mother hurrying up the stairs behind her, but she didn't slow down. She just wanted to get to her room and throw herself on the bed and cry until she had no more tears left.

How could she possibly have gone and fallen in love with a man capable of hurting everyone she cared about? And that *was* what she had done. She'd realized it the night before when she'd had so much trouble taking off that beautiful ring he'd bought for her for all the wrong reasons. The sad truth had echoed in her head just that afternoon when Petey had talked about her becoming his mom.

She made it as far as the bed, but the hot angry tears had barely begun to spill when her mother sat down next to her and pulled her into her arms.

"Okay, why don't you tell me what's going on?'' Janet asked.

Her gentle reasonable tone had a calming effect on Jenny's distress. "I've made a real mess of things,'' Jenny said, sniffing. "I thought I could work it out with Chance, keep him from doing this, but I've only made it worse."

"How?"

She took a deep breath, then blurted, "He said if I'd marry him, he'd settle for my share of the ranch and forget about suing."

Her mother stared at her in shock. "He what?"

Jenny regarded her ruefully. "You heard me. He was trying to blackmail me into marrying him."

"Why, that rotten low-down scoundrel!" her mother exclaimed. "How could he put you in such a terrible position?" Holding Jenny's shoulders, she searched her face. "You turned him down, didn't you? You told him to taking a flying leap, right?"

Jenny nodded. "More or less."

"When?"

"Last night."

"Well, good. The whole idea is absolutely ridiculous." She paused and studied Jenny's face again. "It is, isn't it?"

"Of course," Jenny said, then sighed.

"Oh, no," her mother whispered. "You've fallen in love with him, haven't you? Harlan told me he'd seen all the signs of it, but I thought it was just wishful thinking."

"I don't know, maybe," Jenny admitted brokenly. "God, what a mess!"

Janet stood up and began to pace. "Maybe not," she said thoughtfully.

"Mother, I know that tone of voice. What are you thinking?"

"I'm thinking that Chance Adams would never have made such an outrageous proposal if he wasn't at least half in love with you, too."

"No," Jenny said bleakly. "I think this was just part of his revenge. He got me all tied up in knots when he intended all along to sue for half of everything we owned. If I'd said yes, he probably would have abandoned me at the altar just to make his revenge complete."

"He didn't sue until today," her mother reminded her. "After you'd said no. Maybe he's simply trying to force your hand, show you he means business."

"This isn't about me," Jenny said adamantly. "It's about White Pines. It always has been. He came to town to get revenge and now he has, or at least he's put the wheels in motion."

"I'm not convinced of that," her mother insisted. "I think there's more to it. Do you mind if I go down and tell the others what's been going on?"

Jenny resisted the idea. She knew, though, they had to be told. In the end she was forced to admit as much, but she didn't want her mother stuck with the dirty work.

"Give me a few minutes to get my act together and I'll tell them," she said finally. "They might as well hear straight from the horse's mouth just how big a fool I've been."

Her mother chuckled. "You tell them like that and they're liable to go over there and lynch the guy."

"Why?"

"For hurting you."

The prospect held a certain sick appeal. "Do you really think they would do that for me?"

"These are Adams men you're talking about," Janet reminded her dryly. "Protecting those they love is what they do best."

"So telling them this will stir up a real hornets' nest," Jenny said thoughtfully.

"It's what Chance deserves, don't you think?"

Jenny sank back down on the edge of the bed. "Wait a minute, though. What will it solve in the long run?"

"It may not solve anything," her mother conceded. "But right now I'd like to see him with a bloody lip and a couple of black eyes, wouldn't you?"

"No," Jenny said at once, then changed her mind. "Yes." She sighed. "Maybe."

Her mother chuckled at her indecision. "Well, as much as you and I would take satisfaction in that, I think maybe if we all put our heads together, we can come up with something a whole lot more devious."

"To save White Pines?"

"Of course not," her mother said, waving off the suggestion as if the ranch was the least important issue on earth. "To get the man to admit he loves you."

Jenny's mouth gaped. "Weren't you listening? He doesn't love me."

"Oh, I think he does," her mother countered. "But if he's like most men, he just might not realize it yet."

Chapter Thirteen

Chance walked out of Wilkie's barn after feeding the horses for the night and came to a dead halt. There was a parade of pick-ups coming up the driveway, and unless his eyesight was going bad, each one was driven by an Adams. He guessed they'd gotten the word about his suit.

The decision to file it had been impulsive, made in the middle of the night when Jenny's rejection had cut deep into his heart. He'd put it together first thing this morning after a flurry of phone calls and faxes to an attorney in Dallas Wilkie had recommended.

He kept his gaze fixed warily on the approaching trucks. Despite the implications of that convoy, he felt more exhilarated than frightened. It was all finally going to come to a head right here and now. He'd suspected they wouldn't wait around to settle things in court.

He walked toward the fence around the corral, propped a booted foot on the bottom rail and waited. His pulse hammered in his ears.

All his planning and scheming had come to this. The irony, of course, was that with every scheme he'd mentally concocted he'd found himself losing just a smidgen of his heart to a prim and prissy schoolteacher of all things. An Adams.

And that wasn't the way it was supposed to be at all. He was supposed to be immune to all these conniving Texas relations. He was supposed to be completely focused on his goal.

And for a brief while he had actually been able to view Jenny purely as a means to an end, but something had happened in recent weeks that scared the dickens out of him. She was rattling him, leaving him tongue-tied and sweating and aching so damned badly, he needed a dozen cold showers to relieve the tension. Last night had been the worst.

Petey wasn't helping matters, either. For some reason or other, his son had fallen under Jenny's spell, too. Last night of all nights he had talked about her nonstop and actually had the audacity to offer the two of them his blessing.

In the middle of the night, aching for her, Chance had realized he couldn't have gone through with using her to get the ranch even if she'd said yes. He hoped he'd have the chance to tell her that. A look up the road suggested that his prospects for living long enough were iffy at best.

Seven men, all bearing shotguns, emerged from those trucks. He recognized Harlan and Duke and guessed that the others were Luke, Cody, Jordan and a couple of the grandsons. What were their names? Harlan Patrick and Justin. They were young enough to look both eager and uncertain at the same time. It was a dangerous combination in a man armed with a gun. Chance kept his gaze fixed on the two of them as he waited to see who in the group would speak first. Naturally it was Harlan who stepped forward.

"Chance," he said, regarding him with obvious regret, "I'm mighty sorry to be here under these conditions."

Chance tried to ignore the vague sense that he'd disappointed someone whose respect he'd wanted. "It was something I owed my daddy. I made him a promise the day he died," he explained. "I had no choice."

"We always have a choice, son."

"Yeah, right. Were you going to sit down with me over dinner one night and work out some arrangement to turn over some of your land?"

Harlan shook his head, his expression filled with sorrow. "Sooner or later we would have done exactly that. We'd have talked, worked something out to rectify the injustice you believe was done to your father. But we're not here about White Pines, boy. This is more important."

Chance swallowed hard. An uneasy feeling began nagging at him. What could be more important between them than the fate of the ranch? "If you're not here about White Pines or the suit, what's this about?"

"It's about Jenny," Harlan told him.

Chance's heart slammed against his ribs. Had she told them about his proposal? Had they made the obvious link between her refusal and his initiating the lawsuit? He never would have done it if he hadn't spent all night stewing over her rejection. He'd wanted to get her attention, not punish her. He'd wanted her over here today herself, shouting and fussing and making a deal. Judging from the glares of the men standing before him, he'd gotten not just her attention, but the whole damn family's. He'd miscalculated once again. Just as it had been years ago, all the power and the decision making rested with Harlan Adams.

Well, there was nothing Chance could do now except face the music. He brought his chin up a defiant notch.

"What about her?"

"You hurt her," Harlan said coldly. "You tried to use her in a fight with me. I warned you about that. Nobody hurts my girl. Nobody."

Chance could have tried to explain, tried to appease him. Instead, he responded with pure bravado. "What do you intend to do about it, old man? Shoot me?"

"That's mighty tempting, but it'd be too easy," one of the sons said.

"Cody..." Harlan warned in a low voice.

"Sorry, Daddy. I just wanted to make sure he realized we weren't here as window dressing."

Harlan almost smiled at that. "Chance is a smart man. I doubt he'd make a mistake like that."

"If he's so smart, why'd he go and hurt Jenny?" one of the younger boys demanded, his trigger finger moving nervously. "He made her cry. I've never seen her cry before." He sounded both awed and dismayed.

"Now that's a good question, Justin," Harlan said. He looked at Chance. "Care to give us an answer?"

Chance figured his best shot was to try to bluster his way through. "Are you sure you've got all the facts straight about this? I asked the woman to marry me, didn't I? She's the one who turned me down."

"You were using her," Harlan reminded him coldly. "What did you expect?"

Something about this whole situation didn't feel quite right to Chance. He could understand these men being furious about being served with legal papers. He could even see them getting bent out of shape if he'd deliberately hurt Jenny, but she hadn't been hurt when she'd walked away from him the night before. She'd had the upper hand all evening long. It had been her decision to go.

Or had he missed something? He'd convinced himself during the night that he didn't have the capacity to touch her in any way. She'd been willing to walk away, hadn't she? If she'd cared for him at all, wouldn't she have taken a risk on the future by accepting his proposal and working on the details of their relationship later?

"You know, men, as much as I respect the fact that you all stick by Jenny, it seems to me that what goes on between the two of us is just that—between the two of us."

"Not anymore," Harlan said grimly. "You turned it into a battle that drew the rest of us in when you dangled a marriage proposal in front of her as a way of getting a share of the ranch. It stopped being personal right then and became business."

"What exactly does that mean?"

"It means I want you to steer clear of her and settle this ranch thing with me, Luke, Cody and Jordan. I want you to stay so faraway from her you'll only be a dim memory."

Chance stared at him incredulously. "You're forbidding me to see her?"

Harlan shrugged. "That shouldn't be a problem, should it? After all, you were just playing games with her head, weren't you?"

There was no way to answer that question without landing in even hotter water. Chance, however, really hated being told who he could and couldn't see. He especially hated the prospect of not seeing Jenny again. If he'd had to choose between her and the land... Well, thank goodness, it hadn't come to that. Not yet, anyway.

"What if I tell you to forget it?" he asked. "What if I tell you that I'll see her when and if I choose to?"

His uncle didn't look nearly as distraught at those words as Chance had anticipated. In fact, he almost looked as if he'd been expecting it.

"Then I'll go back into court with a response to this suit that will destroy forever any good impressions you had of your daddy," Harlan said.

Chance swallowed hard at the implacable note in his uncle's voice. There wasn't a doubt in his mind that Harlan would do exactly as he'd threatened. Nor, at last, was there a doubt in his mind that the old man had the ammunition to do it. Oddly enough, none of that mattered anymore, not as much as working things out with Jenny. He doubted, though, she would ever trust his motives or him. He supposed she even had a right to hate his guts, but it was her right, not her daddy's to dictate.

"Well?" Harlan asked. "What's it going to be?"

"I'll stay away from her," Chance said at last. Then he allowed himself a slow confident smile. "But only if Jenny tells me herself that's the way she wants it."

"We're telling you," Cody said. "And we're the ones you need to listen to."

"Sorry," Chance said. "It has to come from Jenny."

His uncle met his gaze evenly. "Fine. You follow us on back to White Pines and she'll tell you to your face."

Chance wasn't sure he wanted to risk it just now, especially not with the entire family looking on, but he couldn't see he had much choice.

"I'll be right behind you," he said.

They actually waited until he'd climbed behind the wheel of his truck before they got into their own pickups and headed back down the driveway. He noticed that one of the trucks, the one with the two boys, waited and fell into place behind him. No prisoner had ever been more carefully escorted.

On the short drive to White Pines, Chance wondered just what he was going to say to Jenny or why the heck it mattered to him so much that she not push him out of her life forever. All he knew was that the prospect of never seeing her again left a huge empty space inside him.

"It's not going to work," Jenny declared for the hundredth time since her father and the rest of the men had left to confront Chance. "Telling him he's to leave me alone won't exactly break his heart. All he cares about is the ranch."

"If that's so, we'll know soon enough," her mother said calmly.

Jenny sighed. "Tell me again exactly how we'll know."

"Sweetie, just count the trucks coming up the driveway. My hunch is there'll be one more than the number that left here."

"And that will mean?" Jenny asked.

"That Chance insisted on hearing straight from you that you never want to see him again."

"Well, if you ask me, all that proves is that he doesn't like to lose," Lizzy piped up.

"My sentiments exactly," Jenny murmured.

"Wait and see, you two. I think this plan Harlan came up with is ingenious."

Lizzy groaned. "Mom, you think everything Daddy does is ingenious. You're prejudiced."

Their mother did not appear to be the slightest bit annoyed by the accusation.

"Wait and see," she said again with quiet confidence.

"Well, I just hope and pray Daddy has all his meddling out of his system by the time I'm ready to find a man and settle down," Lizzy announced. "I'd like to handle the details of my courtship myself."

"Then you were born into the wrong family," Jenny said dryly.

She crossed the living room to the window and peered outside again, searching for a stirring of dust on the long winding driveway that would indicate that the confrontation with Chance was over and the troops were returning home. Lizzy came up beside her.

"Daddy won't let you down," she said softly.

"I know." Jenny nodded. The only real question was whether or not Chance would let her down, whether he would choose the ranch over her. She'd been so sure on more than one occasion that her feelings for him were reciprocated.

"Isn't that Daddy's truck?" Lizzy asked urgently, pointing to a tiny moving speck in the distance.

Jenny's heart skipped a beat. "Looks like it," she said. "And there are Luke's, Cody's and Jordan's behind it."

"Damn, I wish I'd thought to get those binoculars from Daddy's office," Lizzy said. "Isn't that another truck behind them?"

"It's probably Justin's," Jenny said.

"No, no, his is behind the one I'm talking about." She turned and grinned at Jenny. "It's Chance. It has to be."

Jenny pressed her nose against the windowpane to get a better look.

"Jenny, you're fogging up the glass. In a minute we won't be able to see anything," Lizzy complained.

"Have either of you considered just going out on the porch to meet them?" their mother inquired.

"And look anxious? Are you kidding?" Jenny snorted. "That would defeat the whole purpose of this crazy stunt. Chance has to be convinced I don't care if I ever see him again."

Lizzy rolled her eyes. "Do the words straightforward and honest mean anything to anyone in this room?"

"Of course," her mother said. "But when it comes to men, sometimes a winding road will get you to the destination a whole lot faster than a straight line."

"Whatever that means," Lizzy said.

"It means you shouldn't put all your cards on the table at once," Jenny explained. "Keep them guessing."

"And you—Miss Direct and to the Point—subscribe to this?"

Jenny grinned. "Not really, but I have been persuaded today to listen to my elders and learn from their wisdom."

"You'll see," her mother said. "Very soon, I suspect."

Sure enough, within minutes the pickups were slamming to a stop in front of the house, and sure enough, Chance's was among them. It looked as if he'd been surrounded by a posse. He didn't appear overjoyed.

"Mama," Jenny said worriedly, "what if they just kidnapped him?"

Janet chuckled at her concern. "Does anyone look bloodied? Any shotguns raised?"

"No, but Chance does look as if he'd like to murder someone," Jenny concluded after studying his grim expression. "I think maybe I'll just slip out the back door and head for…" She shrugged. "I don't know, any place but here."

"Jenny Runningbear Adams, don't you dare leave this room," her mother commanded, getting gracefully to her feet. "I think I'll tell Maritza that our guest is here and she can serve tea now."

Jenny and Lizzy exchanged glances as their mother left the room.

"Tea?" Lizzy said. "Since when do we have tea?"

Jenny chuckled. "Maybe that was another lesson we missed. Maybe it goes with bulldozing a man into admitting he's in love with you."

Before her sister could respond, booted footsteps sounded in the foyer. Jenny glanced nervously at the door.

"Go on in, son," her father was saying. "Ask her what she wants."

"Is it vital I do it with an audience?" Chance asked.

The low rumble of his voice raised goose bumps on Jenny's arms.

"What do you think, Luke? Cody?" That was Harlan again.

"I suppose he can be trusted to be alone with her in her own house," Luke responded.

"Besides, Jenny's got better aim than half of us," Cody said. "I ought to know. I taught her to shoot."

After that things happened very quickly. Maritza brought in a tray with teacups, a teapot and tiny sandwiches and cakes. Her mother shooed Lizzy from the room, and then Jenny was alone with Chance. The gaze he fixed on her was hot enough to brand cattle. She forced a bright smile.

"What brings you by?" she asked.

"As if you didn't know."

"I have no idea. Last I heard, you failed to convince me to go along with your scheme to get a chunk of White Pines, so you were suing for half the ranch.'' She gestured toward the tray Maritza had left. ''Care for some tea?''

He eyed the china cups suspiciously, as if he expected them to shatter at first touch. ''I don't think so.''

Jenny shrugged and poured herself a cup, more for something to do than out of any desire for tea. She added several lumps of sugar and a splash of milk for the same reason. She would have tossed in a shot of liquor if any had been nearby.

Chance's scrutiny turned speculative. ''You nervous about something, darlin'?''

''Why would I be nervous?''

''I thought maybe you didn't feel so good about having to lie to me.''

''What lie? Why on earth would I lie to you?''

''If you tell me you never want to see me again, that would be a lie. You know it and I know it.''

She returned his gaze blandly. ''Is that so?''

He'd been standing behind her father's favorite wing chair, but now he moved toward her and sat next to her on the love seat, thigh to thigh. No wonder they called them love seats, Jenny thought. A man and woman crowded next to each other on one of these were forced into a certain intimacy. She could feel his heat reaching out to her. It took all her restraint to keep from pitching herself straight into his arms.

Which, of course, was exactly what he intended.

"Say it," he instructed quietly, his gaze locked with hers.

"Say what?" she murmured.

"That you never want to see me again." He reached out and brushed a strand of hair away from her face, then trailed his finger along her jaw.

Jenny couldn't have spoken two intelligent words, much less the whole lie she was expected to spit out. Her heartbeat was so fast, so unsteady, a cardiac monitor would have labeled it unhealthy—or love.

"Well?" he encouraged.

"Chance..."

"Yes, darlin'. I'm waiting."

Jenny shot to her feet and raced for the safety of the spot he'd vacated behind the wing chair. She clamped her hands on the back so he wouldn't see them trembling.

"I want you to go," she said even as her heart cried out for him to stay.

For a fraction of a second he looked stunned. Then he was on his feet and moving toward her again. A cougar stalking its prey couldn't have looked any more intense.

"Okay," he said softly, "I'll go, but only after one last kiss."

Her pulse ricocheted wildly at the suggestion. "Absolutely not," she said breathlessly.

"Why not? You've kissed me before. This won't be any different. Just a little goodbye kiss between acquaintances if that's the way you want it."

That, of course, was the trouble. He wasn't just

an acquaintance and that wasn't the way she wanted it. She wanted him to plunder her mouth. She wanted him to make mad passionate love to her right on that infernal love seat. One little kiss was more dangerous than he could possibly imagine. It would never be enough.

"No," she said emphatically.

His eyes glittered. "Too risky?"

"Of course not."

"Then prove it. Prove you can kiss me and then tell me to go away."

"Why? What difference does it make whether or not I kiss you? The game's over, Chance. You'll go into court and take your best shot. Maybe you'll win, maybe you'll lose, but you'll have done what your father wanted. You can get on with the business of living your life, instead of his."

"This kiss isn't about White Pines," he told her. "It's about you and me."

"There is no you and me. The fight over the ranch has made sure of that."

"Then I'll give up the fight for the ranch," he said.

Jenny wasn't sure which of them was more stunned by his statement. Chance looked as if he couldn't believe he'd uttered the words. Jenny wasn't sure she'd heard them.

"Damn," he muttered, raking a hand through his hair. "I should have known I couldn't do it."

Jenny smiled, more relieved than she'd ever admit. "Couldn't do what?" she asked innocently.

"Use you to get the ranch."

She shrugged as if that was no surprise. "Never thought you could."

He stared. "Why not?"

"Because it's not the kind of man you are," she said confidently. "I knew you'd never go through with it. It was just a matter of waiting you out until you saw what I knew all along."

"Which is?"

"That you could never do anything to hurt someone you love."

Chance started at the mention of love. "What makes you think I love you?"

"You're giving up on White Pines, aren't you? Why else would a man give up something he wants so badly?"

"Is there anything else you think you know about me, Miss Smarty-Pants?"

"That you're going to ask me to marry you," she suggested, but she couldn't keep a hint of hesitation out of her voice. What if she was wrong? What if he didn't want to marry her? She held her breath as she waited for his response.

"And what would your answer be if I did?"

She grinned. Naturally he couldn't have made a straightforward reply, not a man like Chance.

"Oh, no, you don't, Chance Adams. If I'm going to be saddled with a couple of hellions like you and Petey, you're going to have to do it the old-fashioned way. I want a brand-new, genuine, from-the-heart proposal."

"Will you marry me, Jenny Runningbear Adams? It's you I want."

"Say that again," she said softly.

He hesitated for one long endless beat of her heart, then said, "Marry me and I'll forget about White Pines."

"Why?"

"Because you're more important," he said, and now he spoke without any hesitation at all. "It's a funny thing about land. One piece is pretty much the same as another. It's the people who make the difference. I can make a home wherever you are. I can't make one anywhere without you."

Tears welled up in Jenny's eyes halfway through this pretty speech. "Why?" she asked again, this time in a whisper.

"Because you were right. Somewhere along the way I've gone and fallen in love with you."

"You're sure?" she asked, not quite daring to believe it.

"I'm sure," he said emphatically. "What about you, darlin'? I haven't heard you say a word about what you feel."

Jenny's throat was so clogged with emotion she couldn't manage to squeak out so much as a single word. She settled for rounding the chair and throwing herself into Chance's waiting arms and peppering his face with the kisses he'd demanded and she'd withheld. She added a few more for good measure.

"I can't hear anything," they heard Lizzy whisper from the other side of the door.

"Get away from the door," her mother said. "You, too, Harlan."

"How the heck are we supposed to know what's going on if we don't listen in?" he demanded, sounding thoroughly disgruntled. His voice faded a bit, though, suggesting that her mother had gotten him to move.

Chance chuckled. "It's always going to be like this, isn't it?"

"Worse," Jenny confirmed. "If we get married, you'll be switching from outsider to family member, which means Daddy will assume a God-given right to meddle in your life."

"If?"

"Okay, when."

"That's more like it," he said solemnly. "Petey told me last night he was giving us his blessing. I figure that's too precious to waste."

Jenny smiled. "He mentioned the same thing to me."

"Smart kid," Chance said.

"The brightest," Jenny agreed.

Chance shook his head, his expression one of disbelief. "You sound a whole lot like a proud mama."

"Isn't it amazing what a difference a few weeks makes?"

"A few weeks and the love of a good man," he said.

"That, too." She wound her arms around his waist and fit her body to his.

There were more whispers outside the door, then a thump as if someone had bumped against it. Jenny sighed.

"We might as well put them out of their misery before someone out there gets hurt," she said.

Chance glanced over her shoulder toward the door, then grinned. "Nah," he said. "Let 'em sweat. I have more fascinating things in mind than satisfying your daddy's curiosity."

He edged over to the door and flipped the lock to assure their privacy, then grinned at her. "Come here, darlin'."

Jenny heard the indignant muttering on the other side of the door that indicated her father was aware he'd just been locked out of his own living room. She chuckled.

"That bought us maybe five minutes," she warned. "Daddy has a key in his office."

"Then I guess we'd best make the most of it," Chance said, and angled his mouth over hers.

Jenny lost track of time, lost track of everything except the feel of Chance's lips, the hard warmth of his body. She was about to suggest a test run of the love seat when she heard the spare key rattle in the lock over her mother's protests.

Chance kept his arms looped around her waist from behind and faced the door as her father burst through. Jenny couldn't see Chance's face, but she saw the expression of satisfaction on her father's.

"I guess she didn't tell you to get lost," Harlan said dryly.

"To the contrary, she's agreed to marry me," Chance told him.

"I see."

"Do we have your blessing?" Chance asked, then held up a hand. "No, wait, don't answer that yet. Do you have those legal papers anywhere around here?"

"Right here, snug in my pocket," her father said, pulling them out.

Chance took them from him and ripped them in half. Jenny recalled another legal agreement that had been shredded on another wedding day years before. Her gaze flew to her mother, whose nostalgic smile suggested she was recalling the very same thing.

"Now do we have your blessing?" Chance asked.

Harlan grinned at him. "It was never in doubt, son. Jenny has a way of getting what she wants."

Jenny reached for her father's hand. "Of course I do. I'm an Adams."

"Always will be, too," Chance said. "It's a proud name, don't you think?"

"That it is," her father replied. "That it is."

Epilogue

Jenny had never envisioned herself in a fancy white wedding gown. She wasn't sure why. Maybe it was for the same reason she'd never played with dolls or makeup and had climbed trees and painted graffiti on her daddy's old shed, instead. As a kid, it had been pure rebellion. Standing in the Fort Worth bridal shop, it was pure gut-deep panic.

"I'll look ridiculous," she muttered, even as she fingered the delicate lace and the smooth satin of the samples the shop owner had supplied.

"You'll look beautiful," her mother corrected. "All women look radiant on their wedding day."

"But me? In frills? I don't think so."

Her mother grinned. "Forget the frills, then. Go for simplicity."

Simplicity turned out to be more outrageously expensive than frills, but Jenny stood in front of the mirror in a slim gown that hugged her breasts and flowed to the floor in endless yards of satin, and her breath caught in her throat.

"Oh, my," she whispered.

"I guess you're not a tomboy anymore," her mother said, brushing her cheek with a kiss and squeezing her hand. "You're all woman."

"Do you think Chance will like it?"

"I think you could wear a terry-cloth robe and Chance would like it."

"Mother!"

"Okay, okay, Chance will love it. He'd be a fool not to."

Lizzy grinned. "What Chance will love most is getting you out of it. It has a nice simple zipper down the back, instead of all those tiny impossible buttons."

"Careful, sis. We still have your dress to pick out. I could decide I want you in pink tulle."

"Then you'd have to get yourself another maid of honor," Lizzy shot back. "And all those bridesmaids you're planning on would wind up hating you because they'd have to wear mauve or something to coordinate with me."

"Pink and mauve, the perfect colors for the day before Mother's Day, wouldn't you say, Mama?" Jenny asked.

Janet chuckled. "I think pink and baby blue would be even more appropriate."

"You two are awful," Lizzy declared. "How did I survive growing up around you and turn out so good?"

"You can thank Daddy for that!" Jenny said, laughing. "You're one hundred percent Daddy's little girl."

"Oh, go to—"

"Mary Elizabeth Adams," their mother said. When Lizzy fell dutifully silent, Janet fiddled with the train on Jenny's dress. "I think this is the one, don't you?"

Jenny gazed at herself once more in the triple mirror and slowly nodded. "Oh, yes," she said softly. "This is the one."

For one day in her life, she was going to look every inch a lady. Of course, more than likely, no one in town would recognize her.

"Daddy, did you wear a tuxedo when you married Mama?" Petey asked.

Chance ran a finger around the too-tight collar of his white shirt and cursed the day he'd agreed to wear one for this wedding. "No, son, and don't ever let a woman talk you into wearing one, either."

"But I think you look real handsome. I'll bet Jenny's going to think so, too."

She'd better, Chance thought grimly. He'd put on this monkey suit for her and her alone. Of course, when he thought of the grumbling she'd done when she'd had to go shopping for a wedding dress, he'd figured it was worth it.

It still astounded him how things had turned out. Coming to Los Piños had been the best decision of his life, even if it had shattered forever his impression of his daddy being wronged by a cheating older brother. He'd forced Harlan to tell him the whole story one night when they'd been sipping bourbon and talking about life's astonishing twists and turns. Chance had been saddened by what he'd heard, but at last he'd understood his father. Some of the old Hank had lived on in his father until the very end, enough that Chance had recognized the truth in his uncle's story.

He reached into his pocket and fingered the ruby-and-diamond pin his father had stolen all those years ago. Tonight he would give it to Jenny. Tonight it would be back where it belonged as part of the Adams-family heritage.

"Daddy, I hear the music," Petey said, his voice quivering with excitement.

"Then I guess it's time." He hunkered down in front of his son and straightened his tie. "Looks to me like you were made for a tux yourself, young man. A few years from now every girl in Los Piños will be chasing you."

"Oh, yuck!" Petey declared with a grimace.

Chance laughed. "You'll change your mind." He tapped Petey's pocket. "You have the ring?"

"Dad! You've asked me that a million times."

"So what? Things have a habit of disappearing around you. Give me an answer one more time."

"It's right here," Petey said, dragging it out of

his pocket. "See. I'm not going to mess up, Dad. That's why I'm called the best man."

Chance grinned and ruffled his son's hair, which had been slicked back a little too neatly to suit him. There, he thought. Now Petey looked more like the pint-size scoundrel he was.

"You are happy about this wedding, aren't you?" he asked, also for the millionth time.

"Dad!"

"Okay, okay, I was just checking."

"Can we please go get married now?" Petey asked.

Chance looked at him and grinned. "Yes, son. Yes, we can."

The wedding had gone off without a hitch. In fact, it was the first thing in Jenny's entire life that had.

When she'd spotted Chance and Petey waiting in the front of the church, her heart had climbed into her throat. She'd thought for a minute she was going to burst into tears from sheer happiness. Then she'd looked up into her father's sparkling eyes.

"Ready, darlin' girl?"

"Oh, yes," she'd whispered.

Lizzy, Sharon Lynn and Angela had started the procession. He'd grinned at her and said, "Just one last thing before we walk down that aisle. I may be giving you away to Chance today, but you will always be my darlin' girl. Don't ever forget that."

Tears had spilled down her cheeks and she'd dabbed them away. "Look what you've done," she chided. "You've made me cry. I thought it was only the bride's mother who was supposed to cry."

"In this family we've never done anything according to the rule book," he said. He glanced toward the front of the church. "Looks like your groom might be getting a mite anxious. Shall we put him out of his misery?"

"There are some who'd say his misery will start the minute we finish saying I do," Jenny said.

"Not around me, they won't," Harlan said, tucking her arm through his and taking the first step down the aisle....

Now Jenny was standing in the middle of the honeymoon suite at a very fancy Dallas hotel. In the morning they would fly off to an undisclosed destination for their honeymoon. To her exasperation, Chance had been adamant about keeping the details a secret.

"A man's got to find an edge wherever he can," he'd told her repeatedly. "Something tells me I'll never get one with you again."

Smiling to herself, she resolved to wrangle the secret out of him before the night was over.

"What are you grinning about?" Chance asked, coming back into the suite's expansive living-room area wearing only his tuxedo pants.

"Nothing in particular," Jenny claimed as her gaze zeroed in on his bare chest. How could she possibly think about anything except how desperately she wanted to touch him, to be touched by him? She'd waited so long for this moment, her entire life, it seemed.

He crossed the room slowly. "Have I mentioned that you're the most beautiful bride I've ever seen?"

"Once or twice," she teased, hoping he'd tell her again. She liked hearing it, loved the way his gaze heated when he said it.

He moved closer, close enough for his scent to surround her, but to her deep regret, he didn't touch her. Instead, his gaze locked with hers.

"You are the most beautiful bride I have ever seen, Jenny Runningbear Adams."

"Really?" she whispered.

"Absolutely."

His hands settled on her shoulders, his thumbs touching bare skin at the edge of her gown. Jenny trembled from that oh-so-slight caress.

"You know what, though?"

Jenny swallowed hard. "What?"

"Lovely as it is, I really want you out of this dress."

Her lips curved into a smile. "I would have been out of it hours ago if you hadn't insisted on scooping me up while I was still wearing it and carting me off to Daddy's plane for the trip to Dallas. I had a very expensive, very prim going-away suit I was supposed to change into back at the house."

"Forget prim. It doesn't suit you, at least not around me. You can show it off some other time. I was too anxious to get you to myself."

She touched his face, felt the way his skin burned. "You've got me. Now what?"

He took a step back and Jenny felt suddenly bereft.

"Champagne?" he asked lightly.

This time she was the anxious one. She shook her head. "No champagne."

"A late supper?"

"No food."

He grinned. "What then?"

She shrugged and feigned a yawn. "I suppose we should get some sleep."

"Oh, no, you don't," he said. "I've waited way too long to get you in my arms and in my bed."

"Actually the bed doesn't belong to you," she teased.

"Funny." His gaze locked with hers again. "Come here, darlin'. Turn around."

Heart hammering in her chest, Jenny moved closer, then turned her back to Chance. She felt the skim of his fingers as he found the zipper and tugged it smoothly down. His knuckles burned a path down her spine.

She felt the bodice of the gown fall loose. And then, as the zipper dipped below her waist, all those yards of satin slid into a pool at her feet.

"Sweet heaven," Chance murmured as he turned her around to face him.

The adoration Jenny saw in his eyes in that instant took her breath away. For one long endless moment time stood still. The power of love shimmered in the air, as pure and radiant as anything she'd ever felt in her entire life.

Then, with a single touch of his hand on her breast, it exploded like fireworks into a spectacular barrage of sensation. His mouth was everywhere, tasting, teasing, magical.

And his hands, oh, his wonderful, gentle, persuasive hands slid over her, lingering, tormenting, magical.

The last of the clothes—her lacy lingerie, his slacks and shorts—disappeared in a trail as they worked their way toward the bedroom. It took an eternity to get there. With each step, with each scattered piece of clothing, there was something new to explore, a new sensation to rock them both.

By the time they reached the bed, Jenny's knees were shaking and her heart was thundering like a summer storm.

"I love you," Chance murmured as he settled her in the middle of the huge soft mattress and stretched out beside her. He began exploring her body all over again, as if it were a brand-new experience to be savored.

Jenny thought she was going to shatter into a million pieces from the wonder of it. When Chance finally kneeled above her, when he slowly entered her, filling her, then withdrawing until a scream of protest formed on her lips, only to die with the next thrust, she felt as if she'd finally found what she'd been seeking her entire life. She felt whole, a part of something larger than herself. She felt as if she'd come home.

Much much later, with Chance's arms wrapped tightly around her, she tried to express to him what he'd given her. The words eluded her.

"I feel complete," she finally said. "That's what you've done for me. You've given me my own family and made me whole."

"You've always had a family," Chance said, clearly not understanding. "Your mother, your sister, all those brothers. And no father could love a daughter more than Uncle Harlan loves you."

"I know that. It's just that it was something I had no control over. He didn't choose me to be his daughter. He didn't father me biologically. I was part of the package that came with Mom."

"That doesn't mean he loves you any less."

"No, of course not," she said impatiently. "But you chose me, just me."

He shook his head. "You're wrong about that, darlin'. There was never any choice to make. What I feel for you just is. It's there in my heart and I couldn't deny it."

He reached across her in a movement that brought bare skin brushing provocatively across bare skin again. Jenny's body vibrated with awareness and shivery desire, but Chance had something other than making love on his mind.

"This is for you," he said, and opened his hand.

Jenny stared at the dazzling ruby-and-diamond

pin. It looked old and delicate and more beautiful than any piece of jewelry she'd ever seen.

"Oh, Chance," she whispered. "It's gorgeous."

"It's the pin my daddy took when he left White Pines, the one that came from our Adams ancestors. I want you to have it. I asked Uncle Harlan and he agrees it belongs with you."

Tears welled up in her eyes as he put the pin into her hand. It was yet more evidence of belonging.

"Sorry, there's no place for me to pin it at the moment," he said dryly.

"I don't want to wear it, anyway. I just want to look at it." She stared at the sparkling gems, then met Chance's gaze. "It's like it's come full circle, isn't it?"

"I think nothing on earth would have made my father happier than knowing it was back where it belonged. As much as he treasured this pin and the memories attached to it, I think he regretted taking it away from Los Piños. I've thought about it a lot lately. I'm not as sure as I once was that he truly wanted revenge. I think maybe he just desperately wanted some part of him to come home again to White Pines. I think that's why he was so insistent that Petey and I come here."

Jenny touched his cheek. "Maybe he knew somehow that this was where you'd find your destiny."

Chance smiled. "Maybe he did at that."

* * * * *

Take 4 bestselling love stories FREE

Plus get a FREE surprise gift!

Special Limited-time Offer

Mail to Silhouette Reader Service™

**3010 Walden Avenue
P.O. Box 1867
Buffalo, N.Y. 14240-1867**

YES! Please send me 4 free Silhouette Special Edition® novels and my free surprise gift. Then send me 6 brand-new novels every month, which I will receive months before they appear in bookstores. Bill me at the low price of $3.57 each plus 25¢ delivery and applicable sales tax, if any.* That's the complete price and a savings of over 10% off the cover prices—quite a bargain! I understand that accepting the books and gift places me under no obligation ever to buy any books. I can always return a shipment and cancel at any time. Even if I never buy another book from Silhouette, the 4 free books and the surprise gift are mine to keep forever.

235 SEN CF2T

Name _____ (PLEASE PRINT)

Address _____ Apt. No. _____

City _____ State _____ Zip _____

This offer is limited to one order per household and not valid to present Silhouette Special Edition® subscribers. *Terms and prices are subject to change without notice. Sales tax applicable in N.Y.

PAULA DETMER RIGGS

**Continues the
twelve-book series—
36 Hours—in May 1998
with Book Eleven**

THE PARENT PLAN

Cassidy and Karen Sloane's marriage was on the rocks—and
had been since their little girl spent one lonely, stormy night
trapped in a cave. And it would take their daughter's wisdom
and love to convince the stubborn rancher and the proud
doctor that they had better things to do than clash over their
careers, because their most important job was being Mom and
Dad—and husband and wife.

For Cassidy and Karen and *all* the residents of Grand Springs,
Colorado, the storm-induced blackout was just the beginning
of 36 Hours that changed *everything!* You won't want to miss a
single book.

Available at your favorite retail outlet.

Silhouette ®